VOYAGE OF THE DOGS

VOYAGE OF THE DOGS

GREG VAN EEKHOUT

HARPER

An Imprint of HarperCollinsPublishers

Dedicated to Amelia and Dozer.

They're good dogs.

* * *

VOYAGE OF THE DOGS

ONE

LOPSIDE HOPED TO FIND A RAT.

He sniffed the passageways, and he sniffed the bulkheads, and he sniffed inside the elevators and beneath the food heaters in the galley. He sniffed the waste vents, and he sniffed inside the agricultural dome, aching to catch that familiar rodent scent.

Ratting was one of the most important jobs on the *Laika*, and Lopside was the ship's ratter.

He was named Lopside because one of his ears stood straight up like an antenna, while the other flopped over his eye. He had fierce teeth and a keen sense of smell to go along with a body that weighed no more than a small sack of kibble. His coat of black and cinnamon-brown fur was always unruly, even after a fresh brushing.

"Wherever there's people, there's rats," Roro liked to say. Roro was the ship's agricultural engineer and senior dog wrangler, and she was Lopside's very best friend. "In the days of wooden sailing ships the rats would scramble up gangplanks and skitter across mooring ropes. They'd settle in dark holds, eating away at stores of biscuits. So wherever a ship docked—whether it was a busy port or desert island—the rats would come with it. From dock to ship, from ship to dock, always rats. Rats and people. They even say a rat stowed away on the first voyage to Mars."

But Lopside wasn't just looking for rats. His official job on the *Laika* was to sniff out trouble of any kind. He knew what the ship was supposed to sound like, what noises were normal and what noises could mean a problem. He knew what the decks were supposed to feel like under his paw pads. And he knew how the ship was supposed to smell. He was trained to detect burning odors, the bitter stink of melting wires and overheated power transfer junctions. A fire on a starship could be deadly. So he spent hours every day combing the ship with his nose fully engaged. His body was small enough to squeeze into tight spaces that the human crew had a hard time reaching, and his nose was even more sensitive than a lot of their sensors.

"Hey, Lopside, do you have a spectrum calibrator on you?"

Lopside lifted his nose from the deck plates and stared up into the eyes of Crew Specialist Dimka. He wagged his tail at him and barked, "Sure do."

Lopside wore a backpack with pockets that held an assortment of tools—spanners, radiation probes, calibrators, and anything else the crew members might need. He liked how the backpack made him useful, and the sensation of the straps wrapped snugly around his belly comforted him.

He bit a plastic tab dangling from one of the straps to open the pocket where he kept his spectrum calibrator. Specialist Dimka reached down to grab it and gave him a scritch behind the ears. His hands smelled like lemons and coolant.

"Good boy, Lopside. I'll come by the kennel after my shift to give this back."

Lopside wagged his tail and continued on his way.

The corridors echoed with greetings as Lopside continued his patrol.

"Hey, Lopside!"

"Hi, Lopside!"

"Who's a good boy? Lopside's a good boy!"

He made his way to the agricultural dome, delayed by encounters with more crew members, many of whom insisted on petting him, scritching him, or even giving him treats.

The dome rose higher than a maple tree, a web of support struts with transparent panes of plasteel in between. Solar lamps shone from the ceiling, bathing the dome in a delicious warmth that felt like being wrapped in a blanket. On the ground, new crops sprouted in a field of neat rows, some of them in beds of soil and others in white hydroponic containers of chemical nutrients. Outside, all was stars, like glowing silver fleas against a vast, black void.

Lopside found Roro on her knees beside a mound of fertilizer, planting garlic. Of all his jobs on the ship, his favorite was helping Roro tend the crops that would feed the crew once they landed on Stepping Stone.

He ran to Roro, dropped his pack, and flipped over to expose his belly for a rub. Roro gave the best belly rubs.

"How was ratting today?"

Lopside barked and wriggled happily in the dirt. "It went pretty great. I sniffed the engineering module, command-and-control, and the communications array. I detected no problems."

"Good!" Roro said.

Lopside thumped his tail. He liked praise.

"I didn't find any rats, though," he said, his tail slowing just a little. "But I did get scritches from Crew Specialist Dimka, Med Tech Murph, and a biscuit from Commander Lin."

When Lopside spoke to the human crew, he didn't do so in words, but with barks and gestures and postures. He communicated with the angle of his ears, with the way he cocked his head, with the speed and direction of his tail wags. And the crew members of the *Laika*, from the commander to the most junior assistant engineer, were equipped with translation chips that turned dog communication into human language.

"Sounds like a busy shift," Roro said with a smile. "But try not to overeat. Remember, you're going into hibernation in the morning, and you can't digest treats in deep sleep."

"We still get dinner, right?" Lopside never went hungry on the *Laika*, but he was still always very concerned about feedings.

"Don't worry, you'll get your kibble. Now, do you want to help me work or not? Hand me a thermal probe, please."

"Of course," Lopside barked, rolling over to his feet.

The next morning, the dogs of the *Laika* gathered in the hibernation chamber. They arrived even before Roro, because Champion had ordered them to. Champion was a golden retriever with a coat like polished brass and dark eyes that gleamed with intelligence. On Stepping Stone her job would be search and rescue. On the ship, she served as Commander Lin's assistant and leader of the dog pack.

She strode up to Lopside, alert and confident, and sniffed his muzzle. "You smell nervous. Worried about hibernation?"

"Of course not."

"There's really nothing to be afraid of. It'll be just like taking a nap."

"A six-month-long nap," Bug grumbled. Bug was a black, white, and tan corgi shaped like a squat log with big bat ears. He worked in the engineering module and tried to act like the engineers, who were a cranky bunch, probably because they were tasked with maintaining the ship's important systems and knew what could happen if any of them broke down.

"It won't be like that at all," Champion said, giving Bug a withering glare. "We'll go to sleep and then wake up and it won't feel like any time has passed. Nothing to fret over, Lopside."

"I'm not fretting," Lopside barked. He was the smallest dog of the pack and the only non-purebred, and just because he was, in fact, worried about hibernation didn't mean they needed to have a conversation about it.

"I'm terrified," Daisy said. "I think we're all going to die." Daisy, the Great Dane, was still a puppy, with a head the size of Lopside's entire body and legs like a giraffe's. She worked in cargo, helping move bulky crates. And on the planet, she'd assist with construction.

Bug offered the most reassurance he was capable of. "Hibernation isn't *always* fatal. We *might* not die."

"But we're not going to eat for six months," Daisy wailed. "I'm going to starve."

Daisy took a gallop around the hibernation chamber. She liked to gallop when she was worried. She also liked to gallop when she was happy. Or hungry. Or full. Or awake. The other dogs tried to make themselves smaller to avoid a collision.

Lopside told himself he'd be okay. Yes, hibernation carried some risks, but that was true about every part of space travel. And even though they'd be asleep, the pack would be together. Pack was closer than friendship. Closer than family. And Lopside knew Roro would never put him or his packmates in danger. She was just as much pack as the dogs. Thinking about that helped him feel better.

Besides, hibernation was a necessary part of the mission.

The journey to Stepping Stone was the first Earth expedition outside the solar system, a trip so long that the crew would have to spend part of it in hibernation to save on resources like food and water. In hibernation, they didn't have to eat, they didn't have to drink, and they used less precious energy. The *Laika* had launched from Earth months ago, heading out past the Moon, beyond Mars, dodging the asteroid belt between Mars and Jupiter, moving past the grand gas giants, out farther than Pluto, farther than the Oort cloud where comets were born, out and out until even the mighty Sun was just a pinprick of light. The dogs were awake for all that time, but they would be in hibernation in the deep-space gulf between Earth's solar system and the system of the star HD 24040, 152 light-years away. Eventually, they would land on the star's fourth planet, which Space Operations had named Stepping Stone. There, the crew would erect shelters. They'd farm their own food, and they would explore an entirely new world. If they were successful, more ships would come, and the outpost would grow, and from there, they would launch new missions to even farther stars. The *Laika* was just one small step into a giant leap of limitless possibility.

Of course, the humans couldn't go alone. There had to be dogs. Because wherever humans went, dogs came along. Like rats, only more helpful. Dogs would herd livestock. Dogs would keep watch against the unknown. And, most importantly, dogs would keep the human crew company during the long spaceflight, and on their new home, far away from Earth.

But first they had to get there.

Roro and Medical Officer Ortega entered the hibernation chamber, all smiles and calm smells.

The dogs came over to sniff Ortega, and when Roro sat down on the deck, they piled atop her and rolled around while she scruffled their ears and patted their bellies and gave them her very best scritches. Even dignified Champion grinned with joy.

But when Roro finally stood, Champion sat on her haunches, giving Roro her full attention. Lopside and the others followed Champion's lead.

Ortega helped Roro get the dogs into their hibernation chambers. The chambers were plastic beds with thin foam pads, but Roro packed them with blankets to keep the dogs warm and comfortable. One by one, she patted their heads, scritched their bellies, rubbed their backs, and told them what good dogs they were. She said there was nothing to worry about.

"When you wake up, we'll be so much closer to Stepping Stone," she said. "And you won't even feel that time has passed. It'll be just like you had a good night's sleep."

Roro scratched Lopside behind his floppy ear, his favorite place.

"Will I dream?" he asked her.

"I imagine you will."

"What will I dream of?"

"The same thing you always do: chasing rats."

Lopside thumped his tail.

"Just try not to run too hard in your sleep," she said.

"You'll detach a sensor pad or something."

She gave him another good ear scritch, stroked his back, and shut the lid to his chamber. He heard a soft hiss, and the last thing he saw through the clear plastic was Roro's smiling face.

TWO

LOPSIDE OPENED HIS CRUSTY EYES and stretched his jaws in a wide, creaky yawn. His tongue felt like burned toast, and he had to pee.

Triggered by his motions, the lid to his chamber opened with a puff of air.

He expected to see Roro's face looking down on him, but she wasn't there. And neither was her scent.

Swallowing an uneasy growl, he leaped down to the deck.

"Report," Champion ordered with a clipped bark.

The dogs gathered and sniffed each other's butts.

The dogs could communicate with barks and growls and whimpers and other vocalizations, but nothing told them as much as scent, so sniffing was part of standard mission protocol. The smell of their butts said that they'd all emerged from hibernation in good health. But something wasn't right. The chamber was dark. A single emergency light in the ceiling cast a dim orange glow. Why weren't any of the crew members there to make sure they awoke from hibernation safely? Why was nobody there to greet them hello? To pet them? To give them treats? And where was Roro?

"They must be dealing with a higher priority," Champion barked with confidence. On her orders, the dogs spread out to search the ship for the crew.

Lopside expected to run into a human right away, but after checking the agricultural dome and the crew quarters level, he hadn't run into anyone. That was when a knot started forming in his stomach.

He sprinted to the lifepod docking station, where he found Champion, panting. Lopside didn't have to smell her to know she was upset. Where the lifepod should have been was just a gaping, empty docking ring.

"Did you find anyone?" he asked.

Her tail drooped. The answer was no.

The lifepod was gone.

The crew was missing.

And the Barkonauts were alone.

"I want a full inspection," Champion ordered once all the pack had returned to the hibernation chamber. "Our top priority is determining the condition of the ship. What's working? What's not working? Report back here in one hour. Go," she concluded with a commanding bark.

Lopside broke off in a trot for the environmental systems control module. It didn't take him long to realize the *Laika* was in trouble. Some of the doors weren't closing all the way, as if the door frames had been knocked out of shape. Entire sections of the ship were dark and freezing cold. In some places, the air smelled like rotting garbage. The water tasted weird.

Little blinking lights on the environmental control panel meant the systems that pumped breathable air through the ship weren't working right. Some blinked red, the signs of systems that weren't working at all. Lopside lifted his nose and drew in a deep breath. The air held a lonesome stillness.

Before things had gone wrong, Lopside could nose his way through the ship and catch the scents of dozens of humans. Smells clung to the shoes of crew members who tracked them from different parts of the ship. He used to smell traces of sweat and soap, of coffee and garlic and onions from the galley. He could smell traces of laughter. He could smell homesickness.

Now, the ship smelled empty, and flat, and stale. It smelled lost.

He was nosing beneath the environmental control console when he caught a familiar scent. Before he even knew what was happening, his heart was thudding in his fuzzy chest and his tail started wagging fast enough to generate a breeze.

He'd caught a whiff of Roro.

He could almost see her scent, like a faint red line floating in midair. Nose twitching, he pursued it along a snaking path, concentrating so hard that it occupied almost every cell of his brain. He would not lose the scent.

He followed the trail through the deep whir of the gyroscope tunnel and into the space-suit locker. Twenty-four survival suits hung empty on hooks. No hands filled the gloves. No faces looked out from behind the visored helmets. And next to the twenty-four empty suits was a hook where the twenty-fifth should have been. But it was missing.

He exited the locker and made a right turn, coming upon Passageway Six. And there, he paused.

There was nothing particularly remarkable about Passageway Six. Like dozens of other passageways through the ship, it was a tube-shaped corridor lined in off-white paneling. Just a route from one part of the ship to another. Yet it made Lopside's tail droop. It made his ears lie flat against his head.

This was where Roro's scent was strongest. And it was also where it ended.

THREE

AFTER INSPECTING THE SHIP, THE dogs gathered in the kennel to report their findings.

The kennel was where they ate and slept. Each dog had their own sleeping mat. Dispensers in the walls spit kibble and spouted water, and the dogs could relieve themselves into floor vents that collected their waste, purified it, and recycled it into fresh food and water. There were ropes for tug-of-war, a ball gun that fired rubber balls to chase, bubbles that burst from a nozzle, and plenty of toys to chew and destroy. Most of these things weren't standard gear, but Roro had built them out of spare parts.

Bug gave his report first, standing at attention on his squat little legs, his feet like round muffins.

"We are in a lot of trouble," he barked.

With that, he sat down to show that his report was complete.

Champion did not think it was complete. She didn't growl, and she didn't show her teeth, but Lopside could tell she was seconds from doing both. Apparently Bug noticed, too, because he stood back up.

"More detail?" he asked.

"Yes," Champion said, her lip curling back just the tiniest bit.

"We have no engines at all. No pulse engines, no Tesseract motor. The *Laika* is dead in space."

"We're dead?" Daisy yipped. "We're dead! Dead, dead, dead!"

The other dogs waited while Daisy galloped around the kennel in a panic.

Once she lay panting in an exhausted heap, the meeting could continue.

"The ship's systems are running on battery," Bug said. "But without the engines running, we can't recharge them. All our systems are strained: heat, air, food recycling, gravity . . . It's like the ship is starving but we're still asking it to run."

"How long can the batteries last?" Champion asked.

"I don't know. A couple of weeks? Maybe days? It depends on how much we use them to stay alive."

There was a dark silence as the dogs took this in. Without power, they'd run out of air. They'd run out of food and water. And with the ship stuck in the cold depths of space, they'd freeze to death.

"I've checked the scanners, so at least we know where we are," Champion said.

She moved to the wall and lifted her paw to activate a viewer. A familiar sight appeared: a glowing dot with smaller dots rotating around it. The dot in the center was the Sun. The third dot in was Earth. Home.

"We started here," Champion said, touching her nose to Earth and leaving a wet nose print. "Now, we're here." She touched the viewer again, and another system of dots appeared. This was the star HD 24040 and the planets orbiting it. A small rectangle blinked on the edge of the system: the *Laika*. "We still need to get from where we are now, to here." The final touch of her paw lit up the fourth dot from the star. This was Stepping Stone, their destination.

Champion looked at each dog in turn. They all thumped their tails to show they'd paid attention and understood what Champion had said so far.

They were still 4.7 billion miles from Stepping Stone. It was an enormous distance, but the *Laika* had already traveled more than 150 light-years from Earth. Considering a light-year was the distance a beam of light traveled in one year, and that light moved at a speed of 186,000 miles every second . . . it boggled Lopside's mind to think about. But the important part was this: The Tesseract motor had warped space and brought the ship from the edge of Earth's solar system to the edge of Stepping Stone's. To explain it, Roro had shown the dogs a picture from one of her favorite books. In the picture, an ant crawled across a straight length of string. It was a long way for the ant. But if you brought the two ends of the string together, the distance was much shorter. The Tesseract motor shortened distances in much the same way. But it wasn't safe to use it inside a planetary system, because the gravitational effects could be deadly. For travel *within* planetary systems, the *Laika* relied on her pulse engines.

"With pulse engines, we could make it the rest of the way there in forty-six days," Champion was saying. "Bug, I want you to turn off unnecessary systems to save power. As long as we're adrift, we're using up energy we can't spare. And then start doing whatever you have to do to bring the pulse engines online."

Bug barked, "Affirmative."

"Next," Champion continued, "we'll focus on sending a distress signal back to Earth." Everyone sat up a little straighter. The dogs were trained to solve problems. "One challenge with that: The transmission dish is pointing the wrong way. So we need to get it pointed toward Earth. Unfortunately, the dish's rotation controls aren't working."

"We've got more broken things than working things," Bug grumped.

Champion stared at him. She wasn't a fan of anything that sounded like complaining.

Bug flipped on his back to display his belly. Champion gave it a very soft bite and let Bug get back to his feet. In a more positive tone, he said, "We might be able to turn the antenna dish without the controls if we do it from outside the ship."

Lopside's tail twitched with nerves. He didn't like how this meeting was going. Outside the ship was not a safe place to be. The whole point of the ship was to hold the insides in and the outsides out. Inside the ship there was warmth and breathable air. Outside the ship was only frigid cold and airless vacuum.

"I can go outside," Daisy volunteered, drumming the deck with her paws. "I'd be real good at going outside."

"We don't have a Great Dane space suit," Bug reminded her, struggling to scratch his ear with a rear leg that didn't quite reach. "We don't have any dog space suits at all. But we don't need space suits to go outside the ship. We can use a Rover."

The Rovers got their names from the initials for *Remote Operated Vehicle*. The *-er* part came because Rover was a much better name than Rov.

"Problem," Champion said. "I checked the Rovers during my inspection. The remote operating transmitters are dead."

Bug sighed.

Daisy tried to lick her eye.

But Lopside had an idea. It was not necessarily a good idea. In fact, it was a risky, dreadful idea. But the pack couldn't keep drifting along in a broken ship. They needed help, and contacting Earth was their only chance of finding it.

"I might know of a way we can use the Rover without remote control," he said. He tried to say it brightly, with a happy tail, but Champion smelled right through him.

"You're scared," she said.

Bug and Daisy knew it, too.

"Come on," Lopside said. "I'll tell you my idea in the airlock."

At the mention of "airlock," the other dogs started to smell as afraid as Lopside.

Back when he was still on Earth, Lopside had trained every day for the Barkonauts program. There would be only four dogs on the mission to Stepping Stone, and he wanted to be one of them so bad his brain sometimes broke and he'd go zooming around the training yard, as if his desire to go to space was a rat, and if he ran fast enough he could catch it. But so much of training was about learning to remain calm. It was about learning to focus on new tasks. He mastered new tricks, new commands, new words. He and other dogs sat before control panels with dozens of different buttons, and the trainer would say, "Press the button with three circles." The dogs who pressed the correct button would get a treat. The dogs who couldn't do it were sent to good homes.

They lived very nice lives, with comfortable beds and trips to the park and lots of attention. But they wouldn't be going into space.

Only the best-trained dogs would become Barkonauts.

By the time they got to learning about airlocks and the vacuum of space there were only twelve dogs left in the training pack: Lopside, Champion, Bug, Daisy, and eight others.

"Pretend this is you," the trainer said, holding up a plump link of pork sausage. Lopside started to salivate at the sight and smell of it, and he wasn't the only one. Daisy wriggled, gobs of slobber dripping from her mouth. Champion alone held herself perfectly still, paying more attention to the trainer than the sausage.

Lopside tried to do as Champion did, because she was the best dog in class. But the sausage smelled so good.

"Just like you, the sausage has skin, and the insides are stuffed with meat," the trainer said. "The reason the stuffing stays inside the skin is because there's just as much pressure inside the sausage as there is outside of it. We call this equal pressure. Right now, on Earth, in this room, we are all under equal pressure."

The trainer paused and looked over the pack to see if

the dogs were understanding the lesson. Lopside glanced at Champion and tried to copy her posture and expression, since he figured Champion understood everything.

The trainer walked the sausage over to a table, upon which sat a metal box with a glass door, like a small oven. "This device is called a decompression chamber. But let's pretend it's the *Laika*." He put the sausage inside the box. "There will be air on board the *Laika*, and the environmental systems will keep the air pressure at Earth-like levels. The pressure inside you will be the same as the pressure outside you. Equal pressure."

Champion sat with her eyes focused on the trainer and her head cocked slightly to the side. Lopside cocked his head slightly to the side.

"Now, let's pretend our decompression chamber here is the airlock. The airlock is the one part of the *Laika* that opens to the outside. I am now going to simulate opening the airlock and letting all the air escape into space. Outside the *Laika*, in open space, there is no air. Without air, there will still be pressure inside the sausage, but zero air pressure outside the sausage. Observe."

He flipped a switch, and the dogs watched with rapt attention as a hissing noise filled the room. Very quickly, the sausage began to change. Its skin bubbled, as if it was boiling on the inside, and it started to swell. In seconds, the skin broke, and grease leaked out.

The trainer opened the decompression chamber, plucked out the sausage, and held it up for the dogs to see.

"This is you, exposed to the vacuum of space. This is you if the *Laika* is damaged and loses atmosphere. This is you if you go outside the *Laika* without a space suit. And this is you if you're standing in the airlock when the airlock door is opened."

Meat stuffing oozed.

"So, who's going to stay away from the airlock?"

All twelve dogs raised their right front paws. None of them wanted to become exploded sausages.

"Good dogs," the trainer said.

As a reward for learning the lesson, all the dogs got to eat a piece of the sausage.

FOUR

THE DOGS GATHERED IN THE *Laika*'s primary airlock.

The Rover was there, held down by clamps. It looked like a cross between a small refrigerator and a robotic octopus bristling with screwdrivers, wrenches, plasma torches, flashlights, and grippers and clamps on mechanical arms. Everything you could need to fix things outside the ship.

Champion paced circles around the Rover, inspecting it with her keen eyes and nose.

"The Rover's not a space suit," she said, as if she disapproved of whoever had designed it so poorly. "It was never meant to hold a living passenger."

Bug came to the anonymous designers' defense. "But it can do the job. The tool compartment is pressurized to protect delicate components. And we can squeeze an air recycler from one of the space suits in there to provide oxygen. We can make this work."

Bug tended to see the downside of things, but Lopside could tell he was trying hard to keep a positive attitude. Champion expected nothing less of the dogs, and with the humans gone, she was in charge not only of the dogs, but of the entire ship. Lopside looked at the small compartment on the Rover's back. It was a place to store spare parts and nuts and screws and bolts—things the Rover needed to make repairs. Of all the dogs, he was the only one small enough to fit inside it.

That meant he was the only one who could get a distress signal back to Earth.

He hoped he wouldn't end up as sausage.

Preparations were under way to adapt the Rover for canine extravehicular activity.

Daisy was helping Bug, and Champion was keeping a watchful eye on them both, so there wasn't much for Lopside to do but worry. He went about his normal duties, checking the budding crops in the agricultural dome and patrolling the ship for rats. Eventually, he came to Roro's quarters.

None of the crew had much room to themselves, and Roro was no exception. She had a narrow bunk, with a blanket that she'd brought from home, because things that reminded the crew of home helped comfort them on the long journey. There wasn't anything remarkable about Roro's blanket, except that it smelled like her. Her pillow had a permanent Lopside-shaped indentation, because when he couldn't sleep, he would curl up and inhale Roro's scents and listen to her snore.

He climbed up on her bunk now and buried his head in her blanket. It smelled of farm soil and shampoo, but the scents were faint. He couldn't stand the thought of her smell being gone. It was worse than not being able to hear her voice or see her face. Worse, even, than not feeling her warm hand petting his back.

He jumped down from her bunk and pressed his nose against a touchpad on the wall. With a soft buzz, a drawer slid out. He poked his nose in, and it came into contact with a soft piece of cloth. It smelled like Roro's feet. A sock.

He bit down on it to pull it from the drawer.

With the sock in his mouth, he put his paws up on the window ledge over her bunk and looked out into space. Distant stars glittered like pinpoints against the velvet black expanse. There were unfathomable distances between each star, and trillions of miles between the *Laika* and Earth, and billions of miles between the *Laika* and Stepping Stone. And somewhere out there was Roro. Roro and the rest of the crew in the lifepod.

Lopside didn't know how or when, but the crew and the dogs would all be together again someday, somehow. And the first step in making it happen was contacting Earth for help.

This was his mission, and he would not fail.

Lopside was stuffed in the Rover like a loaf of bread crammed inside a banana peel, sharing the space with a radio and an oxygen recycler. He also had Roro's sock. When Champion first saw Lopside with the sock in his mouth, she cocked her head, about to question and judge him, but after she smelled it and understood that it belonged to Roro, she didn't say anything.

"Let's do a systems check," came Champion's barks through the radio.

Champion and the other dogs remained in the passageway outside, looking through a window into the airlock. Lopside didn't like being so separated from his pack. He already missed their scents.

"Are you breathing okay?" Champion barked.

Lopside took a breath. "Affirmative."

Affirmative meant yes. He could have just said "yes," but Roro used to say "affirmative" instead of "yes" while doing something important.

"Can you see okay?"

Lopside looked out through the tool compartment's transparent, break-resistant shield. He could see the other dogs through the window to the passageway.

He started to pant a little. "Affirmative."

"Are the repair arms working? Maneuvering jets charged? Navigational gyroscope spinning?"

Champion and Lopside ran through checks of all the Rover's systems. Everything was affirmative. Everything, except maybe Lopside. He wasn't sure how affirmative he was.

"Rover systems check complete," Champion announced. She paused. "You know how important your mission is, Lopside. If you can't get the communications dish pointed toward Earth to transmit our message, Space Operations won't know they have to send a rescue mission. They won't know we're alone on the *Laika*."

Lopside swallowed. "Affirmative."

The bark almost got stuck in his throat.

"Airlock doors opening in T-minus ten," Champion said.

T-minus ten was the spacey way of saying something was going to happen in ten seconds. And what happened was this:

The doors slid open.

The clamps holding the Rover in place released with an alarming clanking noise. All the air inside the airlock rushed out in a flood of wind, and the Rover was blown into space with such sudden violence that Lopside couldn't even utter a surprised yip. The Rover somersaulted like a tumbleweed in a hurricane, around and around, end over end. Blood rushed to Lopside's head, and his vision closed to a flickering tunnel of black.

"Do not pass out," he told himself. "You can't complete your mission if you pass out. A good dog would not pass out."

"Steady yourself," Champion ordered over the radio.

"You're tumbling forward and clockwise."

The Rover was steered by a series of jet nozzles that sprayed liquid propellant. Ordinarily, they were controlled remotely, but Bug had removed a panel so that Lopside could reach the jet and repair-arm controls from inside the Rover. Lopside stretched his muzzle forward and nudged two jet toggles. Puffs of silver-white exhaust sprayed out, and the Rover stopped rolling and spinning.

The Rover had come to a halt facing away from the *Laika*, and all Lopside could see was space: a vastness blacker than the blackest night. The raging stars were so far away they were just bright points of light, smaller than a period at the end of a sentence.

Lopside had only ever seen space through the windows of the *Laika*. And even with failing systems, the *Laika* was home. Maybe no longer a safe home, but safer than this. He'd always thought of space as full of planets and stars and galaxies, but now, stuffed into a little can, space seemed like the absence of stuff. Space was so, so empty, like the deepest hole imaginable. And he was falling into it.

He nudged the jet toggles, and the Rover made a half turn.

"I am facing toward the *Laika*," he reported.

The ship was longer than two soccer fields, with a spoon-shaped section at the front where the command-and-control module was housed. With another nudge of jet nozzle controls, Lopside began his journey down the *Laika*'s length, drifting past the transparent dome of the agricultural module. He could make out the green fuzz of sprouting celery and broccoli. Next to the dome was the secondary airlock and the spare Rover unit.

Then came the part of the ship that housed the crew quarters, the kennel, and the infirmary. And then, the lifepod docking station. Lopside knew the lifepod wouldn't be there, but he wasn't prepared for how much it looked like a socket with a missing tooth. This was the last place the human crew had been before they abandoned ship.

Lopside tamped down a whimper and kept going.

"Lopside, report," Champion said. Her barks sounded flat, emotionless, businesslike without her smells and tail and ears and eyes to tell Lopside what she was thinking and feeling beyond her vocalizations. It was like talking to half a dog.

"I'm moving toward the engineering module," Lopside barked back. "All systems are normal. I . . . wait a minute."

Lopside gave one of the jet nozzles a squirt to bring the Rover to rest.

The section of the ship before him should have been a smooth, curving piece of gray metal. But here, the *Laika*'s skin was blackened and crumpled. A section of it was covered with rough, bumpy material, like a crust of dried macaroni and cheese.

He moved the Rover in closer.

"Report," Champion demanded.

"I'm seeing repair foam outside Passageway Six," Lopside said. Passageway Six, where, inside the ship, a bare thread of Roro's smell clung.

Repair foam was used to fix leaky hoses, cracked pipes, any of the hundreds of little things that could malfunction on a journey between stars. Lopside had never seen so much of it.

"There's lots of damage. I think I know what happened to the ship. Something breached the hull. We must have hit something."

It was the worst kind of emergency. A hull breach was a full-on disaster. It was like being struck full-speed by a tram and breaking all your legs. It was like the ancient

Titanic hitting an iceberg and sinking. Only worse. More violent. In a hull breach, everything and everyone could be blown out of the ship. A hull breach could kill an entire crew. It could destroy an entire starship.

The breach must have been why the crew abandoned ship.

"Affirmative," Champion said. "Proceed with your mission."

Lopside nudged the Rover along until he made it to the communications dish at the back of the ship. The shallow bowl of the antenna towered over him, taller than a three-story building. Lopside moved in closer to its base, where a giant gear was supposed to turn the dish to keep it pointing toward Earth. With a couple of nozzle bursts, he brought the Rover to a rest over an access port.

So far, so good.

Except it was getting hot inside the Rover. His own body produced heat, and since the Rover was airtight, the heat had nowhere to escape. He began to pant, and the Rover's transparent plastic shield fogged over, making it hard to see outside.

"Calm yourself, pup," he said to himself, trying to imagine how Roro would have sounded.

It helped, just a little.

He craned his neck forward and rubbed his nose against the shield, managing to wipe away some of the fog but replacing it with wet-nose smear, which was almost as bad.

At the bottom of the dish he spotted the communications port, a socket the size of his paw. This next part of the repair mission was more delicate than just steering the Rover around.

He extended the Rover's arm until it made contact with the socket. The great dish began to turn.

The whirr of mechanical motors and giant moving gears would be loud inside the ship, but noise didn't travel in airless space. Other than his own steaming breath, Lopside heard only silence.

Right now, Daisy was probably barking and Champion was probably telling her to hush. Lopside knew Champion wished she could have fit inside the Rover and tackled the mission herself, because with something so important, she was the only dog she trusted. Lopside wished she were here instead of him, too. He ached to be back inside the *Laika* with his pack. But his mission was only half-completed.

"Champion, I'm plugged into the antenna."

"Do you remember the message?"

Of course Lopside remembered the message. Champion had made Lopside practice it over and over until his throat was sore and his barks came out in weak coughs. "Affirmative," he barked.

"Are you sure? You sound out of breath."

That's because he *was* out of breath. Moisture coated his window, the air felt like a sauna, and he was breathing like he'd just run a race.

"Affirmative on remembering the message," he barked forcefully.

There was a long pause. Champion didn't like to be yelled at. If Lopside had been on the ship, she would probably give him a hard, dominating stare that would make him cower with his tail between his legs.

"You are go on transmission," Champion finally barked.

Lopside took a breath.

He licked his lips.

He barked. "Bark-bark-bark. Woof-woof-woof. Bark-bark-bark."

Morse code was a very old form of communication. People used it even before they figured out how to send their voices over far distances. Before radios. Before telephones. The code used a series of beeps that formed letters of the alphabet. Short beeps were called dots, and long beeps were called dashes. With dots and dashes, you could spell out a message.

The most common message was SOS. Dot-dot-dot. Dash-dash-dash. Dot-dot-dot. A cry for help.

Lopside's dots were short, sharp barks. His dashes were longer woofs.

He continued: "Bark-woof-bark-bark bark-woof bark-bark woof-bark-woof bark-woof. Woof-bark-bark bark-woof woof-woof bark-woof woof-woof-bark bark woof-bark-bark."

It took all that just to say, "*Laika* damaged."

His throat felt like sandpaper, but he kept going.

"Bark-woof-bark-bark bark-bark bark-bark-woof-bark bark bark-woof-woof-bark woof-woof-woof woof-bark-bark. Woof-woof bark-bark bark-bark-bark bark-bark-bark bark-bark woof-bark woof-woof-bark.

"Bark-bark-bark-bark bark-bark-woof woof-woof bark-woof woof-bark. Woof-bark-woof-bark bark-woof-bark bark bark-woof-woof. Woof-woof bark-bark bark-bark-bark bark-bark-bark bark-bark woof-bark woof-woof-bark.

"Bark-woof-woof bark. Bark-woof bark-woof-bark bark. Woof bark-bark-bark-bark bark. Woof-bark-bark woof-woof-woof woof-woof-bark bark-bark-bark.

"Bark-woof-woof bark. Bark-woof bark-woof-bark bark. Bark-woof bark-woof-bark-bark woof-woof-woof woof-bark bark."

And that was it. Lopside had sent all their hopes in that string of barks.

SOS.

Laika damaged.

Lifepod missing.

Human crew missing.

We are the dogs.

We are alone.

With the message sent, he detached from the communications port and began the trip back to the airlock.

Roro would have been proud of him. If she'd still been on the ship, she would have greeted him at the airlock with hugs and scritches. She would have given him biscuits and told him what a good dog he was.

On Earth, the trainers and technicians had nicknamed the pack the Barkonauts, and being called a Barkonaut was the highest praise the dogs ever got. Barkonauts were more than simply smart, more than merely obedient, more than just brave. Barkonauts were dogs who completed their missions.

"I'm a good dog," Lopside thought to himself. "I'm a Barkonaut."

FIVE

AS HE GUIDED THE ROVER back to the airlock, Lopside allowed himself a small morsel of hope. The SOS signal would travel on a wave of twist-space, faster than light itself. Space Operations would hear the message, and they would tell the dogs what to do.

But the message would take days to reach Earth, and then days for Earth to respond. And that was assuming the signal *did* reach Earth. It could get broken up by a high-energy radiation burst or blocked by a dense, unmapped object in space. There were a million things that could go wrong. It was like posting a "Lost Dog" flier on a light pole and hoping the right person saw it.

Lopside knew what being lost felt like. He remembered

when he was just a puppy living with a family in a house at the top of a hill. There was a boy who smelled like chocolate milk and the boy's parents. Lopside remembered learning how to play fetch, and how to scratch at the door when he needed to pee. He remembered bursting with energy and wanting to play all the time, just the way Daisy always did.

It was good.

One afternoon before the boy came home from school, the boy's father took Lopside for a walk. Usually the man didn't do this. Usually it was the boy, or the boy's mother. But this time it was just the man.

They went to a park, and Lopside wanted to run in the grass. He liked the grass because the blades tickled his belly and there were so many smells and sometimes bugs to pounce on. But the man wasn't here to play. He took Lopside to a tree, and he tied Lopside's leash around the tree, and then he left.

Lopside waited. He was sure the man would come back. Better yet, the boy or the boy's mother would come for him.

Minutes went by. And then minutes turned to hours. Nobody came for him.

Lopside barked.

He whined.

He panted and crooned, and he dug at the earth, and nobody came. The leash was like gravity, holding him fast no matter how hard he strained against it.

As scared as he was, Lopside knew what to do. He chewed on the leash, tearing at it with his sharp little teeth, and he kept at it until it was nothing more than frayed, slobbery threads. He bit at it some more, and he was free.

Then he sat by the tree as the sky darkened. He didn't know the way home. If he left the tree, he knew he'd disappear into the city streets and starve or get hit by a tram. Water pattered the ground at his paws. Soon, it was a full rain, the drops like cold bullets. Water streamed off the leaves overhead and soaked his fur. He shivered and whimpered in the mud. But he stayed put. The man would come back for him. Or the boy's mother. Certainly the boy. The boy loved him. The boy often fed him scraps under the table, even though the man yelled at him for it. The boy cleaned the messes Lopside sometimes made on the carpet, when he couldn't hold it in. The boy wouldn't abandon him.

But it stayed wet and dark, and nobody came.

Lopside grew too exhausted to whimper. When he could do nothing else, he looked at the round light in the sky. The clouds parted, and the light shone silver-white, its edge sharper than Lopside's sharpest tooth. Later, Lopside would learn that this was the Moon. The Moon circled Earth like a loyal friend, and it was impossible to think of one without the other. The Moon belonged to Earth, and Earth belonged to the Moon, and they'd been together for billions of years.

Lopside watched the Moon make a slow arc across the sky, and by the time he lost sight of it on the horizon, the sky had lightened from black to gray, and from gray to blue.

He lapped some water from a puddle, and his empty stomach growled. There were a few people in the park now, walking, jogging, riding bicycles. Some even had dogs with them. Lopside was too shy to approach any of them, but he barked and he wiggled his butt and wagged his tail to get their attention. Sometimes, he whined at them. He was asking for help. Some people ignored him. They didn't even turn their heads. Others looked at him. Some smiled. Some waved. None gave him food. None helped him find the boy with the chocolate-milk smell. Nobody stopped.

Not until a woman came jogging up past Lopside's tree. Lopside wiggled and whined at her. She cocked her head to the side, curious. Lopside cocked his head back at her.

She looked around, as if to see if Lopside's people were nearby. They weren't, of course. He knew by now they weren't coming for him.

Slowly, the woman approached.

She bent down and offered the back of her hand. Lopside sniffed it. Her skin was a little darker than the brown fur on top of his head, and she smelled like coffee and sweat. She let him lick her salty fingers.

"You lost, little guy?" Gently, she stroked his wet coat. "Oh, you're cold."

She took a little white towel tucked in her waistband and ruffled him with it. The towel smelled like her.

"No tags, huh?"

As she dried Lopside off, he sensed her making a decision, and Lopside hoped on the Moon, even though the Moon was gone for the day.

"Is it okay if I pick you up?" she said.

It was okay with Lopside.

She gently gathered him in her arms and held him close.

"My name's Roro," she said. "And I think I just acquired a friend."

SIX

DAYS WENT BY WITHOUT WORD from Earth. In another week, Earth and the *Laika* would no longer be in alignment, and the communications window would close. If the pack didn't receive a return message by then . . . Well, best not to think about that. Earth would get back to them. Lopside was confident of that. Or was trying to be.

To save energy, the dogs turned down the heat and dimmed the lights in the parts of the ship where they seldom went. And then, later, they made it darker and colder even where they went often. They dragged their beds close and huddled together in the kennel for warmth.

The hardest thing was dealing with the broken food recycler. They had some stores of Emergency Rations

Pellets, but they didn't know how long those would have to last. So, on Champion's orders, they restricted themselves to one meal a day.

It wasn't a good meal. The pellets were formulated for human digestion and tough on a dog's guts, and Roro said they were really named for the sound people made after eating them: "Urp!" But a single ERP provided a day's nutrition, and they were better than starving.

When the dogs slept, the kennel echoed with the rumbles of their empty stomachs. Daisy, already by far the biggest of them and still growing, suffered from hunger the most, and Lopside would sometimes share some of his ration. He knew Bug and Champion did the same.

When he wasn't helping Bug troubleshoot the pulse engines, Lopside kept busy patrolling the ship, sniffing for burning wires or the hiss of an air leak. And, of course, for rats. It was good exercise for his body. And it was important that he keep doing his job. It was important that he keep being a Barkonaut. Meanwhile, Bug worked on trying to bring *Laika*'s engines back to life. He knew the ship's systems best, and he figured when the meteor had hit the ship, it didn't only breach the hull. It had also probably cracked support struts and snapped cables and shaken power junctions out of place. Each of these small injuries was causing other systems to fail, like a pebble rolling down a mountain and knocking into other pebbles until there's a great big avalanche. Bug spent long hours in the engineering module, all by himself, and Lopside knew it must get lonely there, so he made sure his patrols took him to engineering even more often than usual.

"Hey, Bug," he said, his nose skirting the perimeter of the engine chamber.

Bug was sitting on his haunches, staring up at a control console.

"Lopside. You're just in time to give me a hand. Or a paw. Actually, I need your back."

"Affirmative."

Being a corgi, Bug had been bred for herding cattle. Herding dogs were good at keeping complicated systems like groups of giant cows organized. They were good at deciding what to do when things went haywire, like when a cow got scared by a bee and started a stampede. These traits made Bug well-suited to engineering. But since he was so stubby and short, he had a hard time getting up to the control consoles. Smaller dogs like Bug and Lopside were rare picks for space travel, so they had to try a little harder and be a little more stubborn than the others. They'd learned quickly that only by depending on each other could they do some of the things the other dogs could do, and their partnership had helped both of them qualify for the *Laika*'s crew.

Lopside positioned himself at the foot of the control console and stiffened his legs as Bug climbed on his back. Even with Lopside's help, Bug could barely reach the control panel, and there was some grunting from both of them as Bug scrabbled his way up.

"Uh-oh," he said.

"What's wrong?"

"I think . . . I think there's a problem with the singularity core."

The singularity core was a crucial component of the Tesseract motor, and even though none of the dogs had said it aloud, they all knew Earth might instruct them to cut short the mission and return home instead of going for Stepping Stone. None of them wanted the mission to end in failure like that. Besides, they were in a planetary system now, and activating the motor here was extraordinarily dangerous.

Bug growled with agitation. "The core contains a

micro black hole, so if it goes critical the entire ship could fold in on itself and smoosh us down to smaller than a grain of sand."

"How do we fix it?"

Bug took a moment before answering, and his stress odors grew even stronger. "It's a complex mechanism. Once it's broken, there's no fixing. There's only replacing it."

"There must be a plan. We have a plan for everything." Every problem was supposed to be solvable. That was what the Barkonauts learned in training. Barkonauts were dogs who solved problems.

Bug's ears twitched. "If something happens to the core, there's only one other to replace it."

"That's great!" Lopside said with a tail wag. "Where is it?"

"On the lifepod."

Lopside's tail drooped. "Oh."

Bug sighed. "We have to tell Champion."

"I was going to look for rats in the command-and-control module. I can tell her if you want me to."

Bug's ears shot up, and he wagged his nub tail with gratitude. It was never fun giving Champion bad news.

"You're a pal," Bug said.

Lopside found Champion in the command-and-control module at the ship's bow. The lights were turned down, but Champion's golden fur gleamed in the glare of a tablet screen. Most of the crew carried tablets containing information they needed for their jobs, and also music and games and movies and books for their off-duty hours.

Lopside caught an achingly familiar whiff.

"That's Roro's tablet. What are you looking at?" It wasn't against regulations to take Roro's tablet outside the kennel, but it struck Lopside as a little odd.

Champion shut it off. She sat in Commander Lin's chair, his jacket draped over the back. Lopside knew she would have preferred to sit on it as if it were a blanket, but that would have been improper, and Champion didn't do improper things.

"There aren't any rats in here, Lopside." Champion didn't even look at him. She just stared forward at the round window in front of the module.

"There could be rats," Lopside said, feeling defensive. "Wherever there're people, there're rats."

"Well, there aren't any people here, are there?"

Lopside's eyes felt hot, and his jaws felt bitey. "I still think it's worthwhile to look for—"

"Have you completed your daily inspection of the agricultural dome?"

"Not yet. I came here to tell you about the singularity core. Bug says it's unstable. We can't replace it because the only other one was on the lifepod. Bug says if the core fails we'll be—"

"Crushed to death as the *Laika* collapses down to an infinitesimal point," Champion said. "There's no need to panic."

"I'm not panicking."

"Panicking will only make things worse."

"I said I'm not panicking."

"Hmm," Champion said with a tone of dismissal.

Champion's smell didn't quite match what she was saying. She smelled . . . uncertain.

"Is there anything else?"

"No," Lopside said. "Just . . . I'm sure we'll be okay. We'll hear back from Earth, and then all we have to do is hang on long enough for a rescue mission to find us."

"Of course. But right now I need you to go to the agricultural dome. And I need you to shut off the solar lamps."

She said it so plainly, as if she'd ordered him to turn

off a light in a storage closet, or clean up a spill. But her terse command was so much more than that. It was big and awful.

"I've been monitoring the dome's energy use," Champion went on. "The lamps are a massive drain on the batteries, and they're less critical than oxygen production and heat. We can't afford to keep them running."

Turning off the solar lamps would kill the vegetable crops. They would wilt and wither and turn brown and dead. Arriving on Stepping Stone with a supply of healthy, mature vegetables was part of the mission. Good dogs completed their missions.

Lopside was speechless. A growl formed in his throat, and his tail wagged, but not with happy energy.

Champion had been like this from the very first day of training on Earth. She liked to give orders. She liked to be in charge. She was good at it, Lopside had to admit, but he was a terrier. His ancestors were bred to be independent so they could search for vermin on their own, without needing anyone to tell them what to do.

Shivering with pent-up tension, Lopside turned tail and left Champion alone to glow in the blinking lights.

The first tomato lay cradled like a tiny green marble within the fuzzy leaves of a tomato plant. If given water and allowed to bathe in the warmth of the solar lamps, it would grow plump and red and juicy. Given time, all the crops would burst with vegetables.

Lopside moved to the control panel. He drew a deep breath through his nose and held it. The agricultural dome no longer contained even a ghost of Roro's smell. All that was left was her work, the results of all those long hours she and Lopside had spent together, digging in the dirt to raise crops. There were still seeds in storage, but it would take weeks for them to mature into food-bearing plants after landing on the planet. And who would eat them? Dogs couldn't thrive on a mostly vegetable diet.

That's why Champion's order to shut off the lamps made sense. Without the human crew, the crops weren't necessary. They were a waste of energy.

With a whimper, Lopside pressed his paw to a big, rectangular button and pushed. Overhead, with a soft buzz, one of the solar lamps faded to black like a dying star. Within seconds it already felt colder in the dome.

There were four more lamps, and Lopside killed them all. When he was finished, he sat in the dark between crop rows until the cooling soil chilled his belly.

There was still work to do in the dome. Stasis chambers held the embryos of sheep and goats and pigs and cows. When the crew reached Stepping Stone, the embryos would be grown into livestock for the outpost's farm. All the chamber's status indicators were still glowing green, a little bit of light to comfort Lopside's darkened heart.

He moved on to inspect the EggHab. Glass-doored boxes each held half a dozen eggs, some from chickens, some from ducks, some from geese. The eggs were held in stasis so that they wouldn't hatch until the *Laika* reached her destination. But afterward? The outpost would have whole flocks of clucking, quacking, honking birds. Unless Champion ordered him to shut the EggHab down, too.

And if she did?

Lopside wasn't sure how much longer he could remain a good dog.

He went down the row of chambers, checking the readouts to make sure everything was in order. Things looked fine until he got to the last chamber. The lights were off, the readouts blank. He pressed his nose right up to the glass door and sniffed. Bitter odors of burning plastic and the chemical stink of melted wire insulation snaked into his sinuses.

The now-familiar sensation of dread filled his stomach like a cold rock. The chamber was dead, that much was clear. But what about the eggs?

Two possibilities.

One, the eggs and the tiny, developing chicks inside were done for.

Or two, the eggs were okay, but they were no longer in stasis. Now, it was the same as if they'd been freshly laid. How long before the chickens hatched? He thought back to his training.

Three or four weeks. If kept warm, if protected, if looked after like precious, delicate treasures.

Champion's orders were to notify her at once of any systems failures. And Lopside would do just that.

Right after he finished stuffing the eggs in the pockets of his backpack.

Of course, he couldn't keep the eggs there. They needed more protection than his backpack could provide. So he'd tell Champion after he found a good, toasty place to store them.

Of course, Champion might decide they should eat the eggs, since food was running so low.

So, he'd tell her just as soon as the eggs hatched.

On the other paw, Champion might decide they should eat the chickens for the same reason she might decide they should eat the eggs.

What if Lopside waited to tell Champion until the chicks grew up and started laying eggs of their own? That was the whole point of chickens. They were little food factories.

The only problem with waiting for the eggs to hatch and the chicks to grow up to be chickens and the chickens to get old enough to lay more eggs was that the Emergency Rations Pellets would run out long before then.

So maybe the best thing to do was to keep the chickens secret forever.

It was such a stupid plan that Lopside bit his own tail out of irritation.

Well, he'd tell Champion at some point. But not now.

He found a perfect place in the engineering module to hide them, a dark and cozy corner warmed by heat between two thermal junctions. A pair of crew coveralls made a decent nest.

"I'm going to get you safely to Stepping Stone, little eggs. You're going to grow up to be plump chickens, scratching in the dirt of your new home planet. I promise you this."

A smell wafted into Lopside's nostrils, a mix of slobber and exuberance, and it came with the clumsy slap of paws on the deck.

Lopside hurried to conceal the eggs in the folds of the coveralls.

"Whatcha doing?"

Lopside turned to face towering Daisy.

"Hunting for rats. The usual. It's my usual thing. The usual thing I do. Why? What are you doing?"

"Running around." She pawed at the rubber ball she'd dropped at her feet. "It's my usual thing. You should run with me sometime." She dropped into a play bow, her butt in the air and her tail wagging with hope.

Running sounded like the best idea Lopside had ever heard. It would get him and Daisy out of the engineering module and away from the eggs.

"I would like that, Daisy. I would like that very much. Let's go running right now."

"Okay!" Daisy's tail wagged hard enough to fly off

and punch another hole in the hull. She really, really, really liked to run. Her legs started to vibrate, and slobber ran over her tongue like a waterfall. In an open space, or even in the ship's passageways, this was acceptable and even normal. She was just a colossal puppy. But in the confines of the engineering module, so close to the fragile eggs?

"Daisy, this isn't a good place to play."

But Daisy wasn't listening to anything but the irrepressible buzzing in her head. She threw herself on the ground and wriggled around, smashing into machinery.

"Come on out in the passageways. I'll race you," Lopside barked. His current mission was getting Daisy out of the engineering module and away from the eggs.

Daisy did go running, but not in the passageway. Instead, she careened around the engineering module, colliding into conduits and hurtling over control consoles in a gray blur.

Her paw landed on her rubber ball and sent it rolling right for the eggs. She launched herself to retrieve it, and Lopside leaped to block her, but it was like trying to stop a rocket by throwing a lima bean at it. He bounced off her and landed hard on the deck.

Daisy was too wound up with puppy mania to even

notice. And she was still heading for the thermal junction where the eggs were hidden.

Lopside drew in a painful breath and screamed, *"Don't crush the eggs!"*

Daisy skidded to a halt, her giant paws a fraction of an inch away from a collision with the wadded-up coveralls.

She poked her nose in the nest, then cocked her head at Lopside.

"Eggs?"

"Move," Lopside said, nudging Daisy away. He peeled back the coveralls and nosed the eggs. There weren't any cracks.

"Eggs!" Daisy exclaimed.

"Yes. But it's a secret. Don't tell any—"

"You laid eggs!"

"Shhh, Daisy! I just told you, it's a secret."

But the harm had already been done. Bug's scent entered the engineering module, and then he was next to the thermal junctions, scratching himself with his hind leg.

"What's a secret?"

"Lopside laid eggs!" barked Daisy. "Lopside's not a dog! *Lopside is a chicken!*"

"I'm not a chicken, you big sofa."

Daisy screwed her forehead into a befuddled frown. "If you're not a chicken, then how did you lay eggs?"

"He didn't lay eggs," Bug said. "Those are from the EggHab, aren't they, Lopside?"

With reluctance, Lopside explained the EggHab malfunction.

Daisy still didn't quite understand why they needed to be kept secret, but Bug got it right away.

"Champion might consider them food," he said.

Lopside's jaw felt twitchy. "I know."

"She wouldn't be wrong."

"Will you help me keep them secret anyway?"

"Sure," Daisy said.

Bug fidgeted. He vibrated with a low growl. Lopside knew he was asking a lot. It wasn't just that Champion was lead dog. It was that she was part of their pack. Even when the dogs disagreed, even when they argued, even when they fought, they were still a pack. Packs didn't keep secrets from each other.

"Okay," Bug said at last.

Lopside let out a breath that he hadn't realized he'd been holding.

"Thank you."

Bug grunted and walked away.

Watching him go, Lopside sensed that something had been broken. Something more crucial than any system on the *Laika*.

SEVEN

"**CHAMPION WANTS US IN** command-and-control."

Lopside was deep into a garbage chute, clearing up a waste blockage, and Bug's voice sounded distant in the dark. Champion had picked Lopside for the job since he was small enough to get through the tight space and was the pack's best digger. His paws were sticky with goop, and for the first time in his life, he craved a bath.

"Is it about the—?"

He should have told Champion about the chickens. A good dog would have done so. Who was a good dog? Not Lopside.

Bug cut Lopside off before he could finish the question.

"We got a message back from Earth."

Lopside's heart thudded with hope. There was only one more day before the communications window closed, and with each passing hour, it seemed more and more unlikely they'd hear anything. Lopside had begun to worry that he'd done something wrong when he'd rotated the communications dish and barked the message. He'd begun to worry he'd failed his mission.

He flew from the chute and raced Bug to the command-and-control module.

"We have a message?" he panted as soon as he reached the module. Daisy and Champion were already there.

"Affirmative," Champion said. She rose up on her hind legs to reach the comm systems control panel and pawed a button.

The dogs fell silent as a hiss filled the air.

"Dogs of the *Laika*," came a man's voice, a little crackly, a little twangy. "We have received and decoded your message. We share your sorrow at the loss of the *Laika*'s crew. We have received no distress signal from the lifepod. The lifepod is very small, and space is very big."

"We know that," Lopside said with a growl. "Do they think we're stupid?"

Champion struck a hushing posture. Lopside shut up.

"Sadly," the twangy man went on, "this means there is almost zero chance a rescue mission would succeed in locating the lifepod. We must accept that the human crew is lost and beyond recovery. We honor their bravery and sacrifice." The voice paused. It cleared its throat. "Who's a good dog? You are. You are all good dogs."

And that was it.

Nothing about a rescue mission for the dogs. No instructions on how to repair the failing ship.

Nothing but a useless message, and then a return to the silence of space.

"We're abandoned," Lopside said.

EIGHT

BEFORE DOGS, THERE WERE WOLVES. Wild creatures who hunted at night, who bloodied their muzzles in the carcasses of their prey. Lopside's favorite story was the one about how wolves became dogs, and how dogs and humans became friends. The story was contained in *The Great Book of Dogs*, just one of the many books Roro kept on her tablet.

Before hibernation, Roro would put the dogs to bed every night. She would give Daisy a ball to chew, because Daisy couldn't sleep without one, and she'd scratch Bug behind his ears, and she'd brush Champion's golden coat. Lopside would roll over on his back so Roro could scratch his belly. Then Roro would tell the pack a bedtime story.

Curled up in the kennel, listening to the snores and rumbling stomachs of his packmates, Lopside wished Roro were here to tell him a bedtime story now. He would give almost anything to hear her voice. Or any human voice. Except for the one over the radio telling the dogs they were alone.

Dogs needed human voices, and it was a need that went back thousands and thousands of years, before there were starships or computers, when humans were bound to the planet and lived in caves or shelters of animal hide. But even before dogs, wolves had learned to approach humans, because although the two-legged animals were dangerous, with their spears and arrows, they had something wolves wanted: garbage.

Garbage was food. On the rims of their camps, the humans would toss away scraps of meat, morsels of fat, bones that the wolves could break with their jaws to suck down the rich, nutritious marrow. The wolves took from the humans, but they also gave back in return. They frightened away other predators. When danger approached, they howled and snarled and woke the humans from their sleep. It took thousands of years, but eventually the humans and wolves formed a bond. It was an uncertain bond, and it was a bond that was often broken, but it was a bond.

A few of the wolves became the humans' companions. And over a great, long time, the wolves that lived with the humans changed.

The wolves evolved into dogs.

"Dogs and people," Roro used to say. "It's hard to imagine one without the other."

Back in training, she'd told the pack that as long as people and dogs had lived together, they'd been changing each other. Dogs changed the way people hunted. Dogs changed how people traveled and how they lived. But humans changed dogs even more. They bred dogs with traits they found useful—like the ability to run fast, or to crawl into holes after rodents. Humans came to depend on dogs for all kinds of jobs. There were dogs that could help guide people who couldn't see through busy city streets. There were dogs that could sniff out bombs. Even dogs that could smell a person to detect certain diseases. Dogs were bred for their skills, and for size and coat length and temperament, and for dozens of other traits. As a result, dogs became the most varied species on Earth, from the four-pound Chihuahua to the 250-pound English mastiff.

By the twenty-second century, breeding and training

and genetic engineering had turned dogs into the most intelligent animals on Earth, with the *possible* exception of humans. Technology had given dogs longer lifespans. It had given them the ability to see the same colors humans saw. They were still dogs, but dogs with even more ability to work alongside humans.

Humans used technology to change themselves, too, so they could communicate with dogs better. They invented brain implants that translated dog barks and body postures and even dog odors into human language.

Humans and dogs belonged together. It was a belonging that began with campfires in the dark night and advanced in the light of science. Humans wouldn't be the humans they were without dogs, and without humans, there might have never been dogs at all.

Many of the stories in *The Great Book of Dogs* showed what dogs were willing to do for their humans. Roro read to them about Guinefort, a greyhound who belonged to a knight in medieval France. One day the knight left his infant son alone in the castle (very irresponsible of him, Lopside thought), and when he came home, his son's bedroom was spattered with blood. Thinking Guinefort had murdered the boy, the knight killed his dog with an arrow. Only later did he notice the dead snakes near his son's bed. And his son, alive, in a different part of the castle. Guinefort had fought the snakes off and saved the infant's life. For hundreds of years, people honored Guinefort as a saint and prayed to him as a protector of babies.

Roro read to them of Balto and Togo, just two of the 150 sled dogs who fought through 674 miles of blizzards and temperatures less than fifty degrees below zero to deliver medicine to Nome, Alaska. They prevented the death of thousands of people during an outbreak of the lethal disease diphtheria.

Then there was Barry, a Saint Bernard who rescued more than forty people lost atop the icy peaks of the Swiss Alps.

Lopside sniffed Roro's sock and curled into a tight ball in his bed, trying to get warm. He wished he were like Balto and Togo and Barry, who must have been accustomed to cold and snow and ice. Looking for more inspiration, he nosed through the table of contents of *The Great Book of Dogs*.

His eyes landed on the chapter titled "Laika."

Laika was the first living creature to circle the entire Earth from space. She was a hero, and that was why the ship was named after her.

He navigated to the Laika chapter, but the screen was blank. When he nosed Play, the book remained silent. It always did this. In a cruel twist of fate, the chapter about the dog the pack most wanted to know about, and the chapter that for some reason Roro had never gotten around to reading to them, was missing.

So Lopside listened to the story of Balto and Togo again. It was a good story, even though it wasn't the one he wanted to hear.

When the chapter was over, he lay awake and thought of all the things he'd do with Roro when they were reunited. They would play fetch on Stepping Stone. Roro would scratch his belly and she'd tell him stories. And one day, Roro would tell him the complete story of the brave space dog named Laika. And everything would be all right.

NINE

"THAT'S THE LAST REPAIR," BUG said, tearing off the end of a strip of tape with his teeth. "Either the pulse engines fire or—"

"Or they explode and we all get blown to bits?" Daisy asked.

"Exactly," Bug said.

After days of crawling through the engine compartment, sniffing for every tiny broken component, Lopside and Bug had managed to patch, bypass, or reconnect every conduit and cable and wire.

At least they hoped they had.

Today would decide if the Barkonauts would complete their mission and arrive on Stepping Stone, or if they would fail and die slowly in space.

Lopside transferred the chicken eggs from their nest between the thermal junctions to his backpack. If something went wrong, he wanted the eggs near so he could do his best to protect them.

He joined the rest of the pack in the command-and-control module.

"Let's review the procedure," Champion said from her position in Commander Lin's chair. The other three dogs sat on the deck, looking up at her. "We fire the engines for a fifty-three-second burn. That should get us to orbit around Stepping Stone in a little over forty-six days. From orbit, we switch the agricultural dome into Landing Habitat mode. We detach the LandHab and use its thrusters to make a controlled descent to the surface of the planet. And then, that's it. We'll be on our new home."

Champion said it with so much confidence that Lopside almost forgot what a daunting journey lay ahead. Forty-six days to survive while using almost no energy for environmental systems, while nibbling on meager rations, without any margin for error. And even if everything went as well as it could and they made a successful landing, they'd still be without the human crew.

It wasn't how the mission was supposed to go.

But that couldn't be helped, Lopside told himself. This was the situation they were facing. And for Lopside's part, he would face it like a Barkonaut. Champion looked at each dog in turn. "You've all done very well. Bug and Lopside, I know how much work you've done getting the engines back online. And Daisy, you've . . . you've moved a lot of heavy things. All while under stress, without enough sleep, while hungry. You've all made sacrifices for the pack, and for the mission. I'm proud of you. The crew would be proud of you. Roro would be proud of you."

Lopside didn't understand how Champion could manage to say all that without betraying the slightest hint of a whimper. And when he barely managed to choke out, "They'd be proud of you, too, Champion," he understood it even less.

"Take your stations," Champion commanded.

Lopside and Bug leaped into the side-by-side seats before the engine controls systems panel. Champion remained in Commander Lin's seat. Daisy galumphed up to the front of the module and stood with her paws on the main viewer. Her official job was to look out for obstacles, even though the scanners had already shown a clear path ahead for more than 100,000 miles. Champion knew she liked to look out the window.

"Let's run a check," Champion said. "Propulsion activation."

"Go," Bug said.

"Burn clock."

"Go," Lopside said.

"Looking out the window."

"Go, go, go," Daisy said.

The air was thick with smells. Worry. Concentration. Excitement. Hope.

Champion watched the mapping readout, which showed the little red outline of the *Laika* and, still far across the great void, the green circle of Stepping Stone, following its circular path around the star. The *Laika* was like a stick that needed to be flung over 4.7 billion miles so the planet could catch it. Everything had to go perfectly.

"On my mark," said Champion. Lopside and Bug moved their paws over their control panels. "In five. Four. Three. Two . . ." Lopside was panting, but his paw was steady. "Light it!"

Lopside pushed a toggle forward, starting the fifty-three-second clock. At the exact same time, Bug brought his paw down on the ignition control.

"We have ignition," Bug woofed.

Controlled explosions of energetic nuclear particles burst from the engines at the rear of ship, pushing it into motion.

A great, low vibration shook the deck plates, made its way into Lopside's belly, and jingled his tags. He remembered the sensation from the first time the *Laika*'s engines were fired, when the ship left Earth's orbit and began the journey spaceward. He remembered the tense, eager smells of the crew, and the panting breaths of his pack (except for Champion, who had remained calm and serious). He remembered Roro clapping her hands and smiling as the ship got under way.

The vibration and the instrument readouts were the only ways to tell the ship was moving. It wasn't like riding in a car and watching trees outside go by in a blur. Daisy smooshed her nose against the viewer, her tail whipping back and forth. Lopside envied her. If it had been possible to do without dying, he'd have stuck his head out the window and barked with glee as the ship thundered through space.

Eyes on the clock, Lopside called out the remaining burn time: "Forty-three seconds."

Bug checked his readouts. "Pulse interval holding steady."

"Gravity generators compensating for acceleration," Champion said.

"I like space," Daisy reported.

This was working, Lopside realized. He and Bug had fixed the engines, and the *Laika* was no longer floating like a piece of driftwood at sea, and they were going to reach Stepping Stone's orbit and then land on the planet and fulfill the mission, because they were good dogs.

He was about to call out the thirty-three second mark when a massive jolt seized the ship. A heavy silence hung in the air. Nobody made a sound. Not a bark, not a whine, not a whimper. Lopside was still watching the clock, so he knew the silence lasted only two seconds, but it seemed to stretch for much longer than that.

And then the silence was broken. A great big *WHOOM* shuddered through the ship. There was a deep moan, like some great and vast animal in pain. The floor began tipping to the left. The ship was listing.

"Steady," Champion ordered. "Reports, now."

"I have no engine readings," Bug said. "I think the engines are gone."

Lopside checked his clock again. "Incident happened at thirty-three seconds left to go in the burn. We only had acceleration for twenty seconds." That wasn't enough to get them to Stepping Stone.

"We're losing air pressure," Champion said. There was no hint of panic in her tone, or even any alarm, but Lopside could smell it in all of them like a sick fog.

"I have something to report," Daisy said, still standing with her paws on the front viewer. She spoke without puppy energy, but with a tone of dread, and all eyes turned on her. "I can see debris."

Even from his seat, Lopside could could see jagged pieces of waffle-patterned metal flying past.

"That's exterior cladding from the pulse engine cowling," Bug said with gruff barks.

Debris combined with the loss of engine power and falling air pressure all added up to one thing: an explosion. One that had probably reopened the hull breach, or blown a new hole in the ship.

Champion leaped down from the commander's chair. "You three get to the agricultural dome. It has its own air supply. Take shelter there."

"Where are you going?" Lopside asked.

"We'll need to eat. There's one more bag of ERPs in the cargo hold. I'm going to grab it."

"I'm the cargo dog," Daisy protested. "Let me get it."

Champion gave her a hard, dominant stare. "You're the strongest Barkonaut, and I'm counting on you to make sure Bug and Lopside make it to the dome. That is an order, Daisy."

Daisy licked her lips with stress, and Lopside wondered if she was going to disobey Champion's order. And if she did, what could Champion do about it? Daisy still didn't realize how much more powerful she was than the other dogs, but one day, she would. Today, however, was not that day. She tucked her tail between her legs, bowed her head, and said, "Yes, Champion."

Champion turned tail and raced to the command-and-control module door. Before exiting, she stopped to glance back at Lopside and Daisy and Bug. "We're still a pack," she barked. "And we'll survive as a pack."

With that, she ran off alone.

The overhead lights flickered as Lopside, Bug, and Daisy raced down the passageway. The lights were among the ship's most basic systems, and if they were malfunctioning, it meant the *Laika* was in worse trouble than ever.

"My fault, my fault, my fault," Bug kept repeating with panting breaths. "I'm the engineer. I was in charge of fixing the engines. I must have done something wrong. I must have left a connection unfused, or missed a coolant leak, or . . . or—"

By now he was no longer running forward but in circles.

Lopside stopped to turn around. "Bug, I sniffed out leaks and helped you fuse connections. Maybe it's my fault."

Daisy, already many yards ahead of them, galloped back.

"NOBODY CARES WHOSE FAULT IT IS. CHAMPION TOLD ME TO MAKE SURE WE GET TO THE DOME, SO STOP TALKING AND GET RUNNING!" she roared.

Her barks were massive and ferocious and so startling that Lopside almost peed. Bug began sprinting forward again with Lopside right behind him. But when they got to a fork in the corridors, Lopside skidded to a stop.

Daisy looked like she was going to roar again, but Lopside cut her off before she could begin.

"Keep going," he said. "I have to get something."

"But Champion told us—"

"She told us to shelter in the dome, and that's just what I'm going to do. Just as soon as I fetch what I need."

He could tell Daisy was going to stand there and argue with him, maybe even pick him up by the scruff of the neck, and then he'd be helpless, dangling from her mouth and getting slobbered on while she trotted along.

"Here," he said, releasing his backpack. "Take the eggs to the dome. The little chickens are depending on you."

"But Lopside . . . ," Daisy whined.

"You can take me to the dome, or you can take the chickens. You can't take both."

Daisy reluctantly bit the strap to pick up the backpack. With her mouth now occupied, she wouldn't be able to physically stop Lopside from continuing on.

Her eyes pleaded, while Bug looked at Lopside, confused.

"I'll get to the dome," Lopside promised.

He didn't wait for a response from his packmates. Instead, he sped down the left branch of the passageway as though his life depended on it. And it did. In fact, all the dogs' lives depended on him getting to the kennel to retrieve one of the most important items on the ship. But he wasn't sure his packmates would understand why it was worth risking so much for.

His ears picked up a whistling sound that got higher and louder the farther he got, and by the time he reached the kennel, airflow rustled his fur. That could only mean one thing: The ship was leaking air. Had the old breach reopened, the one he'd seen from the Rover, patched with repair foam? Or had the exploding engines opened a new breach? Champion had said she was heading for the cargo hold. That was in D-Module, way back near the ship's stern, far too close to the engineering module and the engines. He could see it in his mind: an entire bulkhead missing, a bag of ERPs spinning in space and spilling pieces of kibble, winking points of frozen water vapor, and Champion tumbling like a tiny bird in a cyclone, coated in frost, dying.

Lopside rushed into the kennel to grab what he'd come for: Roro's tablet. It contained useful information. The ship's technical manual. A celestial map charting the route from Earth to Stepping Stone. But to Lopside, the most important thing it contained was *The Great Book of Dogs*.

The pack needed those stories. Lopside needed those stories. He needed stories of dogs who were heroes. Not all the stories had happy endings, but they still somehow made Lopside feel better. Sad stories could do that, he supposed. They helped him know that he and the other dogs of the *Laika* weren't the only dogs to ever be in danger and afraid. A sad story could be like a gentle scritch behind the ears. It told him that he was not alone.

And somewhere in the book's memory was the story of Laika, the Russian space dog. Her story *had* to be in there. Lopside was convinced that knowing how Laika had accomplished her mission would help him and the other Barkonauts complete theirs.

TEN

LOPSIDE CHARGED DOWN THE LAST passageway to the dome, blinking against bits of dust blowing in his eyes. What had started as a breeze was now a brisk wind. The *Laika* was losing atmosphere, and it was getting worse. Lopside tried not to think about his packmates getting blown out into the vacuum of open space, twirling like leaves amid a constellation of frozen water droplets.

He gasped in the thinning air and made a last push down the corridor. When he arrived at the agricultural dome he found Bug and Daisy huddled in the dark. The dome was supposed to be their last refuge, but it didn't seem very welcoming or safe. The only illumination came from the dull red glow of an emergency light over the doors. He dropped Roro's tablet on the deck and came over to smell his crewmates. They smelled like dread.

Equipment and provisions lay scattered on the deck: some tools, a tank of emergency repair foam, medical supplies, and random pieces of survival equipment. But where was Champion?

"She said she was going for a last supply run," Bug said, anticipating his question. "But it's been more than ten minutes."

He didn't say anything about the wind rustling their fur. The dogs knew what it meant: Even in the dome, air was escaping, drawn into the vacuum of space through a hole somewhere in the ship. The dome had its own environmental systems, but unless they sealed it off from the rest of the *Laika*, it would eventually lose all its atmosphere.

"How much time do we have?" Lopside asked Bug.

Bug gave the air a calculating sniff. "Thirty minutes maximum. Maybe only twenty."

"We don't seal the dome until Champion's back," Lopside said.

Bug and Daisy barked affirmative.

A minute passed in the dark, and another, and then another.

What would Champion do if Daisy or Bug was missing? What would she do if Lopside hadn't made it back from his trip to the kennel?

He didn't have to think about it for long.

"I'm going to look for her," he announced.

"You can't go back out there," Bug protested. "There's four hundred yards of passageways and five decks between here and the cargo hold. Even if you find Champion, you'll never make it back."

"We can't just leave her to die," Lopside growled, his hackles rising.

"I didn't say we were going to. I'm going to take the waste chutes to the cargo hold."

Lopside turned to a black rubber flap on the wall. Every part of the ship had a waste chute for garbage, and to keep smells the humans found unpleasant from permeating the whole ship, they were tightly sealed. It was possible the chutes would retain their air supply longer than the rest of the *Laika*.

"Good idea," Lopside said. "But I'm going."

"No. It's my fault the engines blew up. It's my fault Champion had to go on supply runs. This is my responsibility."

Before Lopside could argue, Bug broke into a sprint for the flap. He looked ridiculous, running with his short legs and muffin paws, but he managed to pick up a lot of speed. And so, when he leaped at the flap but couldn't jump quite high enough, he crashed headfirst into the bulkhead with great force.

"Ow," he croaked, slumped on the deck.

Daisy galloped over. "Are you okay?"

"Do I smell okay?"

Daisy subjected him to a thorough nosing. "You smell fine."

"Good," Bug said. "But, ow."

Daisy gave Lopside a very serious look. "You take care of Bug, Lopside. I'm going after Champion, and nobody's going to stop me."

The giant Great Dane held her head high. With powerful, dignified steps, she moved to the flap and stood with her front paws against it. Her massive hip muscles flexed as she leaped through it . . . and got stuck halfway. Her rear legs kicked air. Her tail whipped madly for a few seconds before drooping.

"Uh-oh," she said, her voice muffled.

"I kind of figured that would happen," Lopside said to Bug.

Bug wagged in agreement.

Daisy managed to extract herself with a great deal of thrashing and whimpering and was about to make a second attempt when Lopside spread his legs and puffed out his chest. He lifted his tail straight out and stiff. "We're wasting time and we're wasting air. I'm going for Champion. Bug, you work on getting some heat and light in here. Daisy, you lick Bug's head until it stops hurting."

Daisy's tongue left a sodden trail from the tip of Bug's nose to between his ears.

"Bug. If I'm not back in twenty minutes, you know what to do."

Bug knew. He would have to seal the dome. It was the correct procedure. But Bug refused to say "affirmative." It frustrated Lopside and even made him angry, but he loved Bug for it.

Ordinarily the chutes were odorless. Swarms of insect-sized cleaner bots were supposed to take care of any spills and traces of bacteria and sticky bits that didn't make it all the way to the secondary airlock to get blown out into space. But the stink of rotten food and poo clogged the tight space. It was a wonderful smell—Lopside liked the smell of garbage as much as the next dog—but it was yet another reminder that the *Laika* was dying.

He had no light to see by, but he knew the chute well—he'd gone ratting and troubleshooting through the entire system before.

The rush of air outside grew louder, telling him he was close to an area of the ship near the breach. Sharp hammer blows startled him enough to propel his heart into his throat. Debris outside the chute must be striking the bulkheads like missiles. He imagined Champion facing a shooting gallery of escaping air and projectiles, and he hurried.

It was when he stopped hearing anything at all outside that he began to lose hope. No air movement. No impact strikes. Not even the usual mechanical hums and whirrs that he hadn't noticed until they fell silent. What did it mean? Had all the systems in this part of the ship failed? Had all the air outside the chute already escaped? Had everything been blown into space? Including Champion?

He'd followed the chute far enough to have made it

to the D-Module. A few more feet and then a left turn, and he'd reach the opening into the cargo hold. He didn't know what he'd do then. If he opened the hatch, he might expose the chute to vacuum. All the remaining air in the chute would escape. Yet *not* opening the chute could mean leaving Champion to die.

Maybe the human crew had faced a hard decision like this. Maybe they'd had to choose between saving themselves or saving the dogs. Maybe they'd had to run, even though it meant abandoning the pack.

What a choice, with no right answer. It made Lopside feel a little sorry for them.

He nudged his head against the flap, pushed through the chute opening, and dropped to the deck of a passageway. Bits of dust skittered across the ground. He squinted against flying grit and raced toward the cargo hold. His lungs couldn't get enough oxygen from the thin air, and a headache brought dark spots to his vision, but he ignored them and pressed on.

When he turned a corner, he spotted a form in the distance. The hatches in this section were heavy steel doors that closed vertically from ceiling to the floor. The cargo hold hatch was down, but something was jammed at the bottom, preventing it from closing completely. It was hard to make out in the dim light, but in his heart he knew what was caught by the door.

He approached and sniffed. It was Champion. And she wasn't moving. Before her lay a sack of ERPs.

"Champion!" he barked. "Champion, wake up!"

Champion didn't respond.

He nudged her with a paw. Then scratched her. Then drummed on her head with both paws, barking her name over and over.

Lopside thought he'd already imagined the worst things that could happen. He'd even lived through one of them—being left behind in deep space by Roro. And everything he and the other dogs had done since then had been about preventing the next worst thing, which was failing to complete their mission. Stepping Stone was still out there, waiting for them. And now they might not even survive.

But if they were going to die, Lopside had thought they'd do it as a pack. They'd die together. He thought of Champion struggling to get back to the dome. He thought of her crying for her packmates, unheard. He thought of her all alone in the dark. It was too much to bear, and not knowing what else to do, he opened his jaws wide and sank his teeth into the scruff of Champion's neck.

"RAAAARRR! What are you doing?"

"Champion! You're alive!" Lopside buried his nose in her fur.

She showed her big, angry eyes and her fierce, white teeth. "I thought I told you to shelter in the dome with Bug and Daisy."

"We did. But when you didn't come back—"

"When I didn't come back you should have obeyed my orders and sealed off the dome."

Lopside contemplated biting Champion again.

"I thought you were dead."

"I thought I was, too." Champion sounded weak. "Report on Bug and Daisy."

"They're fine. Now get out from under that hatch and let's go. We're losing air."

"Can't," Champion said. "I'm stuck."

Lopside took a closer look. Her left rear leg was squeezed between the deck and the hatch.

"Can you crawl your way out?"

"No, I tried that."

"What about pulling with your front legs and pushing with your rear legs?"

"That's what crawling *is*. Since you're here, you might as well make yourself useful. Take the ERPs to the dome."

"I'm going to lift the hatch."

"I gave you an order, Lopside."

"I know. I am disobeying your order. Hmm, now let's see, if I can just wedge myself under the hatch and lift . . ."

He lay on his belly and shimmied his nose through the gap between the bottom of the hatch and the deck. Sick, green scents of pain wormed their way into his nostrils.

"Champion, your leg's really hurt."

"I noticed, thank you."

"Okay," Lopside said. "Okay, my mission objective is to get you free and back to the dome. Okay." He pushed up with all his might, willing his neck and back and legs to be strong enough to lift the hatch, but after several seconds of effort, the hatch didn't budge, and he realized he'd need ten times Daisy's strength to lift it.

He wiggled back out, panting. "That didn't work," he reported.

"Affirmative," Champion said. She sounded dismal.

"Why are you stuck, anyway? The obstruction detector should have triggered the release mechanism when the hatch closed on your leg. The hatch should have opened right up.

I guess after the accident that punched a hole in the hull and prompted the crew to abandon ship, and us blowing up the engines, some things on the *Laika* stopped working as perfectly as we'd like them to. Don't you think, Champion?"

There was no answer.

"Champion?"

Nothing.

So Lopside bit her again.

"OWWWWW!" Champion barked. "What is *wrong* with you?"

"Sorry. I thought you were dead again."

"Well, stop trying to bite dead dogs."

"Well, you stop losing consciousness. Okay, let's think through the problem. The release mechanism isn't working, so we need to fix it."

"Or you could follow my orders, grab the sack of ERPs, and go back to the dome."

"Nope."

"Do you even know what an order is?"

"I'm a Barkonaut. Of course I do. Now, how do I access the release mechanism? I wish Bug was here."

"Bug is back in the dome. With Daisy. Where you should be."

"The dome, right! I remember helping Roro trouble-shoot a sticky hatch in the agricultural dome. The release mechanisms use grade-four lubricant, which smells like"—Lopside's nose twitched as he sniffed the air—"olives!"

He followed the scent to a wall panel beside the hatch. "Yep, definitely smells like olives."

"The mechanism is behind the wall, Lopside. You'll never get to it."

Lopside ignored her and began scratching at the wall. Terriers were known for digging. They were bred to follow rodents into their dens and claw the earth until they found their prey. Right now, the release mechanism in the wall was his prey, and Lopside would not quit until it was exposed. Champion would not die in an airless corridor. Especially not since it was Lopside's fault she was even here. The engines had blown up because of some burned-out switch or disconnected junction. Lopside was the *Laika*'s troubleshooter. He should have found the malfunction.

"Lopside, please. Go back to the dome. This is not your responsibility. This is my fault."

All of a sudden, Lopside liked the way this conversation was going.

"Don't be so hard on yourself," he said with great generosity.

"I'm the one who gave the order to fire the engines. I'm the lead dog. Being in charge means you're responsible for everything that happens on the ship, good or bad. Especially the bad. Commander Lin taught me that."

"Well, it's hard to tell what's going to happen when there's a big hole in your ship."

"Yeah," Champion said. She sounded really down.

"And, look, it's not like you make a lot of mistakes. Your record is pretty good."

Actually, that was an understatement. Lopside couldn't think of a time Champion had made a mistake. Sometimes she gave orders that he didn't like, but they were never the wrong orders. In training she must have gotten nine times the number of treat rewards that Lopside got. He didn't mind that she was better than he was at everything. He just minded that she was *so* much better.

His claws had barely made a scratch on the wall, and he found himself getting resentful again.

"Champion," he muttered. "Perfect Champion."

"What do you mean 'perfect'?"

He was a little startled to realize he'd said it aloud.

"Perfect . . . like . . . the way you are. Perfect."

"It doesn't sound like a good thing, the way you're saying it."

Now Lopside felt bad. For a dog who should be focused on rescuing a packmate, he was pretty busy being resentful of her.

"Of course perfect is good. Perfect is . . . well, perfect."

Champion didn't say anything.

Lopside could smell her getting weaker. She needed to hold on, and Lopside needed to keep her alive until he got through the wall and fixed the hatch release mechanism.

But how?

What would Champion do if Lopside were injured?

She would keep him awake.

"Did I ever tell you how when I was a puppy I was abandoned by my family and I got tied to a tree and it rained and I saw the Moon and then Roro found me and that's how I became a Barkonaut? Did I ever tell you that, Champion?"

"Yes."

Lopside had no recollection of ever telling Champion so much about his past. "Really? When did I do that?"

"Just now."

"Oh."

There followed an awkward silence.

"Do you want to hear it again?"

"No, thank you, I still remember it from the first telling."

"I'm trying to keep you awake. So you won't die."

Champion said nothing in response.

"Champion?"

"I'm still here," she said, in a hoarse bark.

"You need to stay awake, Champion. Tell me *your* life story."

"I don't feel like telling you my life story."

"Would you rather die instead?"

"Of course not."

"Then stay conscious and tell me." Lopside kept digging.

"I was a search-and-rescue dog," Champion said.

Lopside already knew this. "And?" he prompted.

Another pause. Clearly, this was a tale Champion didn't want to tell.

"*And?*" Lopside said again.

"And I was being trained to find lost campers and hikers

in the woods. I loved the woods." Her voice grew distant. "There were foaming white waterfalls, and pools so clear you could stand on the shore and count the rocks on the bottom. And so many trees . . . You should have smelled them, Lopside."

Lopside tried to imagine it, here in this tight space flooded with stale air and scents of fear and injury.

"I was just a puppy then. Nearly my full size, but still a puppy. Clumsy on my feet, but I could run for days on end. I wouldn't quit until I found my scent, and you could put a moose carcass with the gorgeous stink of death in my way, and I still wouldn't be distracted. I was the best dog in my class."

"Of course you were," Lopside said.

Champion went on, ignoring him. Or maybe she hadn't heard him. Maybe she was just talking to herself now.

"One afternoon my handler took me out of the kennel and made me smell a blue jacket. They told me it belonged to a boy who'd wandered off from his family's campsite. He'd already been lost for hours, and it would be nightfall soon, and it was cold, and he didn't even have his jacket. The woods were dangerous. Maybe not as dangerous as space, but dangerous enough to kill a human boy in one night. So, my handler and I joined the search. We had a big area to cover, and there were a lot of scents. Deer, badgers, skunks—you name it. But I did it, Lopside. I found the boy's scent. Just a thread of it, but enough."

"And so you found the boy?"

"It was dark by then, no moonlight, and nothing but treacherous paths. I was pulling at my harness, trying to follow the scent, but my handler kept me back. He told me we'd done all we could that night, and that we had to go back to our base till sunrise."

Champion's barks trailed off, and Lopside barked her name to keep her awake and going.

"So you went back to your base till morning. And then you found the boy? Champion? What happened next? Champion!"

"No," she said with a start. She'd fallen unconscious. "No, I didn't go back to base. I broke away from my handler. I knew the boy was close by. I knew I could find him. And if we waited hours for the sun to rise, who knows what might have happened to him? Like I said, it was a cold night, and he didn't even have a jacket."

"You disobeyed your handler's order," Lopside said, astonished.

"I disobeyed an order," Champion admitted. Lopside could hear the shame in her voice.

"But at least you found the boy, right? You saved his life, so you were still the hero?"

Lopside's nails were worn ragged from digging, but the labor was finally starting to pay off. He'd dug runnels in the wall panel deep enough to sink his teeth into. He bit into the runnels and closed his jaws as tightly as he could.

"The boy was never in danger," Champion said with a trace of a growl. "He was a volunteer. The whole thing was a training exercise. If I'd gone back with my handler like I was ordered to, I would have been petted and scritched. They would have given me treats, and I would have earned my search-and-rescue certificate. But they don't want dogs who can't follow orders. They don't want dogs who think they know better."

The panel was coming loose, but the labor was draining. There wasn't enough air. Icy spikes pounded into Lopside's skull, and his lungs ached. If it was this bad for him, he knew it was worse for Champion.

He released the panel from his jaws to take a quick breath and asked, "So what happened to you?" He resumed his effort, worrying the panel like a caught rat, moving his neck back and forth as if he was trying to break its neck.

"Roro happened. She was looking for dogs to recruit. Dogs who could solve problems without always needing a human handler. Dogs who *didn't* always follow orders. And dogs who think they know better. Dogs like you."

The panel broke free. Lopside let out an excited yip and examined the release mechanism, a black box the size of the card decks the crew sometimes played with. A white hose dangled nearby, dripping fluid that smelled like olives. The hose was about as big around as the metal-ringed socket on the side of the box.

"I see the problem," he reported. "I can fix it. I think."

He bit gently on the hose and tried not to swallow the fluid dripping into his mouth. Grade-four lubricant might smell like olives, but it tasted much more foul.

"There's not enough time," Champion said, her voice reduced to a rasp. "You listen to me. I am your commander, and I am ordering you to get back to the dome."

Lopside didn't bother saying anything. Champion didn't need a dog who could follow orders. She needed a dog who could act on his own. She'd practically said it herself.

Lopside inserted the hose into the socket. There was a *gloop-gloop* sound, and then a humming noise, and then a startling *KERLUNK*, and finally, a joyous *SHRRRUFF* when the hatch lifted up.

Lopside let out a celebratory yelp.

Champion only stared at him through drooping eyelids.

"There's still a long way back to the dome," she said. "And we're still losing air. And I'm pretty sure my leg is broken. Go, Lopside. Go now."

"I am disobeying your order."

Champion sighed. "How like you."

"Yes," Lopside agreed, licking her wounded leg. "And how like you."

ELEVEN

THE FIRST FEW HOURS IN the agricultural dome were a time of healing but not resting. Daisy licked Champion's wounds clean and tore pieces of cracked wall panel to shape a splint. It turned out she had a talent for first aid. Meanwhile, Lopside and Bug tried to figure out how long they could hold out in the dome.

For water, the dogs could drink from the hoses that irrigated the crops. For food, they had only a scant supply of Emergency Rations Pellets left. Lopside had made the choice to drag and push and cajole Champion through the garbage chute instead of hauling the last bag of ERPs Champion had risked her life for. He spared a guilty glance toward the crop rows, where he'd dug out a shallow nest for the chicken eggs and covered them with heating packs he'd pilfered from the medical supplies.

But before they ran out of food and water, they would run out of power. They'd turned one of the solar lamps back on, but just enough to provide a little bit of light and a stingy amount of heat.

Using Lopside's back as a stepping stool, Bug scrambled up on the dome's main control panel. He spent a few minutes examining the readouts, and Lopside could tell he didn't like what he saw.

"I'll give you the good news first," Bug said. "Most of the dome's systems run independently from the rest of the ship's systems. The dome is designed that way so that when it detaches to land on Stepping Stone, it can still function. We have gravity, and the dome's air recyclers are working. As long as we don't venture out, we have air."

"What's the bad news?" Champion cut in, limping over.

"The usual thing," Bug said. "We're still running the batteries dry. The mission plan was that when we reached Stepping Stone and the dome separated from the *Laika*, the batteries would keep it going until its solar cells started soaking up energy from Stepping Stone's sun."

"And we're too distant from the star to get solar power," Lopside said, saving Bug the trouble.

Champion's eyes looked strong, but her tail sagged. "We have to conserve those batteries. We'll run on absolute minimum power from now on. Maybe . . . somehow . . . we'll figure out a way to get closer to the star."

"We have to keep the dome heated or we'll freeze," Bug said. "We need gravity, because the dome's not designed to be a zero-gravity environment. There aren't enough straps and pawholds to keep us from just floating around all over the place."

Champion turned to him. "What else can we cut to save energy?"

"The freezers," Bug said, bowing his head to avoid meeting Lopside's eyes. "They use a huge amount of energy. We'd save a lot of battery power by shutting them off."

Lopside felt heat rising to his head. Losing the crops was one thing. But this was a step too far. The freezers contained the embryos of sheep, goats, pigs, and cows. When the *Laika* landed they were intended to be as important a part of the outpost as the crew and the crops.

"Shut off the freezers and we lose the livestock," he said. "The cows. The sheep. All of them."

Bugs ears flattened. "Would you rather lose Daisy and Champion?"

Daisy looked back and forth, from Lopside to Bug.

"Bug," Champion said, her tail drooping sadly. "Go turn off the freezers."

Bug took a step toward the freezers, and in a flash, Lopside was in front of him, his muzzle wrinkled in a snarl. He felt ancient instincts welling up in him. An urge to solve this with fangs, to latch on to Bug's jaw and take him to ground, to tear into his soft throat, the way he would a rat's belly.

A powerful woof snapped him out of it. "Stop!"

It wasn't Champion. It was Daisy.

She was dancing with nervous energy, her tail a wagging blur. "Stop fighting. We shouldn't fight. We're a pack. Aren't we still a pack?"

Her outburst was enough to knock the violent urge out of Lopside, but his paws still tingled with anger.

"Of course we're still a pack," Champion said with steady calm. "Of course we are. What if . . . what if we put this to a vote?"

Lopside's heart continued to hammer, but a little bit of the tension left his muscles.

"Okay," Bug said. "Lopside?"

"Let's be clear what we're voting on," Lopside said. "It's not just whether we keep the freezers on. Our mission from the beginning has been to establish an outpost on the planet. We're voting on whether we keep trying to complete our mission or not. Barkonauts are dogs who complete their missions. We're voting on whether we're still Barkonauts. And if we're not Barkonauts, we're just a bunch of lost dogs."

Lopside couldn't read Champion's expression. He couldn't even read her smell.

"Then we vote," she said.

Bug planted his little round paws firmly on the deck. "I'll go first. We can't complete any mission if we're dead. I vote we turn the freezers off."

"And I vote we keep them on," Lopside barked back.

Daisy bowed her head and tail. "Do I have to vote?"

"No," said Champion.

"Then I don't want to. It's . . . it's too much."

That left Champion. Lopside knew she would make the difficult choice, the one that he would hate, but the one that held the best hope of keeping them alive. And knowing that, Lopside felt like an abandoned puppy, tied to a tree in the rain. He'd come so far, billions of miles across space, only to end up right back where he'd started.

Champion struck a commanding pose. Even wounded, famished, exhausted and battered, she managed to look magnificent. She took a breath, and Lopside prepared himself to say good-bye to his hope of completing the mission.

"I vote we leave the freezers on and keep the livestock alive," Champion said. "It's the right thing to do."

Lopside gaped at her. "But . . . a minute ago you ordered Bug to shut them off."

"I ordered Bug to do it because I couldn't face doing it myself. That's how I know shutting them off is the wrong thing to do."

Bug relaxed his posture. He came over to sniff Lopside's butt to make the peace between them official.

"Then it's settled," Champion said. "I'm going to see if there's anything around here we can use for beds. I don't want to sleep on cold deck plates." She limped away.

Lopside almost let her go, but Champion was wrong. Things weren't settled. Not as long as Lopside was still keeping a secret from her.

"Wait," he said. "There's something I need to show you."

He led her to the crop rows, where a silver thermal blanket covered the eggs.

"Good," Champion said, misunderstanding. "At least we have one blanket to lie on."

Lopside took a corner of the blanket in his mouth and peeled it back to reveal the heating packs. Champion cocked her head, still not getting it, until Lopside moved the packs aside.

There, safe and toasty in the dirt, lay the six eggs he'd rescued from the EggHab.

He dipped his head and tucked his tail. "I've been hiding these from you," he said. "I've been a bad dog."

Champion looked from Lopside to the eggs and then back at Lopside. Awkwardly and painfully with her splinted leg, she lowered herself to her belly and ever so gently nudged the eggs with her nose.

"Chickens," Champion said at last. "Do Daisy and Bug know about this?"

"Don't blame them. I made them promise not to tell."

"Hmph."

"Please don't order us to eat them," Lopside pleaded, starting with a bark that became a high-pitched whine of begging.

Champion remained silent a long time. Then, "We'll let them hatch," she said.

"And once they hatch?"

"We'll help them grow up into chickens."

Lopside wagged his tail and rolled over to offer his belly in gratitude.

"Don't thank me. Raising chickens was part of the outpost's mission. Since we've decided to remain Barkonauts, we have to do everything we can to fulfill the mission."

"But I should have trusted you," Lopside said. "I shouldn't have kept anything secret from you. That's not what Barkonauts do."

"Hmph," was Champion's only response. She looked at the eggs, and she looked around the dome. She looked everywhere but at Lopside. When she got back up and limped away, Lopside noticed her tail was tucked.

TWELVE

THE PACK HUDDLED TOGETHER ON a plastic tarp that served as their bed. It wasn't much, but it was better than lying on the hard deck or the chilled farm soil. To keep their spirits up, they listened to stories from Roro's *The Great Book of Dogs*. Lopside still hoped he could figure out how to find the full story of Laika, the first space dog, somewhere in the book's memory.

They'd heard all the other stories multiple times and contented themselves by relistening to old favorites, like the story of Bobbie the Wonder Dog.

Before he was Bobbie the Wonder Dog, he was just Bobbie, a collie mix belonging to the Brazier family of Silverton, Oregon. When the Braziers took a cross-country road trip to Indiana, they brought Bobbie along. It was a fun adventure. Bobbie enjoyed sticking his head out the window of the family's land-based vehicle and smelling air redolent with wildflowers and prairie grasses and desert sand warmed by a hot sun. The world was filled with more varied wonders than Bobbie had ever known, and the family was happy they'd decided to bring him along.

Until they reached a fueling station in Colorado. That's where Bobbie was jumped by a trio of aggressive stray dogs. Even though Bobbie ran off, the Braziers weren't worried. They were sure he'd be okay, and he would return soon to the fueling station.

But he didn't.

Maybe he would turn up at the house in town where the Braziers were staying.

But, no, he didn't.

The Braziers searched for him. They asked the locals if anyone had seen him. They put advertisements in the paper-distributed news source. But there was no word.

Days went by, and eventually, the Braziers had to begin their journey home without Bobbie. They knew they'd probably never see him again.

But Bobbie didn't know that.

He walked.

He sought out bare traces of the Braziers' smells, and the smell of their vehicle. He couldn't have known it, but every night the Braziers stopped at fueling stations along the road, leaving behind a few molecules of scent. And once Bobbie found those traces, he kept going.

He swam across rivers. He walked down back roads. He crossed high mountain passes through winter chill and snowstorms.

Six months later, the Braziers' daughter was walking down the street back home in Silverton. And there, halfway across the country from where they'd lost him, she spotted Bobbie. He was thin, starving, his paws raw and his nails worn down to nothing, but Bobbie ran to her, crying and yipping with excitement, his tail flapping in a blur. That night Bobbie feasted on steak and whipped cream, back home with his family.

In all, he had walked 2,500 miles, in the worst weather, over punishing terrain, armed with nothing more than a good nose and an overpowering desire to be with his family.

The morning after the Barkonauts listened to the story

of Bobbie the Wonder Dog in Roro's book, the *Laika* crossed the nine-hundred million-million mile mark of the mission.

To equal that distance, Bobbie the Wonder Dog would have had to repeat his journey 360,000,000,000 times.

THIRTEEN

AN EAR-GOUGING SHRIEK, LIKE A tooth scraping metal, startled the pack awake.

Lopside was up on all fours in a flash. "What was that?"

Champion winced and struggled to get up with her wounded leg, but Daisy gently used her weight to keep her lying down.

All four dogs sniffed, noses twitching, trying to scent out the source of the noise. Except for the smells of urgency coming from himself and his packmates, Lopside didn't notice anything out of the ordinary. But when he looked up at the dome, he spotted a thin white line in the transparent ceiling, like a scar. The shriek rang out again, and the scar lengthened.

"There's a crack in the dome," he said with a sense of horror that bordered on wonder.

Bug grunted. "If the dome's support struts got shoved out of shape, the plasteel panels have been under stress since then. I guess we're lucky the dome hasn't cracked before now."

"This doesn't feel lucky," Daisy said.

It seemed like a cruel thing to happen. They'd survived being abandoned by the crew. They'd lived through a hull breach and an engine explosion. But if the dome shattered, they were dead.

Champion nudged Daisy away and rose shakily to her feet. "Suggestions."

"The freezers," Lopside said. "We can hole up in there."

Champion shook her tail. "They're not airtight. If the dome breaks, we'll be just as dead in the freezers as here."

"Also, we'd freeze to death," Bug pointed out.

"The secondary airlock, then," Lopside suggested. But even as the barks left his mouth, he knew that wasn't a solution. The secondary airlock was a tight space, barely big enough for a Rover and two dogs, let alone four. They'd run out of air in hours.

Another shivery noise came from above, drawing a dreadful yelp from Daisy.

Lopside titled his head to look at the fissure at the crown of the dome. "Maybe we could seal it with emergency foam. We just need to figure out a way up there."

"How?" Bug said. "The ceiling is forty feet up."

"I can make it," Daisy said. She jumped but only reached a couple of feet in the air. "I just need practice."

"What if we fashioned something like . . . like a cannon?" Bug said. "A dog cannon. And we used the dog cannon to shoot me to the top of the dome with a tank of emergency foam." Bug's nub of a tail vibrated. He really liked his own idea.

Champion leveled her gaze at him. "Do you know how to make a dog cannon?"

"Well, no."

"Does anyone here know how to make a dog cannon?"

None of the dogs spoke up, though Lopside had to admit that the thought of firing Bug from a cannon held a certain appeal. But they needed an idea and they needed it now.

"What if we shut off the gravity?" Champion said.

"One of us could drift up to the top of the dome with a tank of emergency foam."

Daisy took another galloping leap. "I bet I could jump pretty high without gravity." She rolled onto her back and wiggled in the soil with enthusiasm. "I can do it! I can save us! Let me save us!"

She smelled like plant fertilizer and she was drooling again, but Lopside realized their lives depended on her.

The emergency foam tanks were designed for a human user to sling over their shoulder by a strap, and they were operated with a handheld nozzle.

"Daisy's big enough to haul the tank, and another one of us will have to aim and control the nozzle," Lopside said.

Champion nodded. "So that's me and Daisy, then."

The other three dogs looked at her and her broken leg. Her ears went limp; she got the message. She was in no shape for a zero-gravity ordeal. That left Bug or Lopside to manage the nozzle.

Champion made her decision. "Bug, you'll work the gravity controls. Daisy, Lopside, the rest is up to you. Affirmative?"

"Affirmative," they all said together.

Daisy said it with great cheer, her butt shaking her

tail so hard with excitement that if they could harness its energy they wouldn't have to worry about dead engines and draining batteries.

She rolled one of the foam tanks directly beneath the dome fissure, then pushed her bread-loaf-sized head into the loop of the strap and squirmed through it.

Lopside examined the nozzle. It had a tapered metal end and a lever. He'd have to operate it by holding it in his mouth and biting down on the lever. His jaws were strong, but not wide, and it would be a stretch.

All the preparation took precious minutes, but it was necessary. The dome could crack open at any moment, but they only had one chance to get this right, and slamming their bodies into the crack or hitting it with the tank might be a fatal mistake.

"Take your stations," Champion ordered.

Lopside envied her calm. She was as steady as ever.

Bug used Champion's back to boost himself up on the control panel.

"When I shut the gravity off, all you have to do is jump," Bug explained.

Daisy gave him a serious stare. "Do not turn the gravity back on until we're safely on the ground. Because if you do, then Lopside and I will fall from the top of the dome and go splat on the deck and you would be a very bad dog. Affirmative?"

"Affirmative," Bug answered, raising one of his stubby white paws over the gravity control. "Here we go, on my three. One. Two. *Three.*"

He brought his paw down.

At first, Lopside noticed nothing different. But then his floppy ear, the one that always hung over his eye like a wilted leaf, slowly rose.

"Lopside," Daisy said, awestruck. "You're not lopsided."

"Never mind that," Champion barked. "Jump!"

Daisy sprang with a mighty leap, and the two of them shot up like overinflated helium balloons.

On reflex, Lopside paddled his legs as if he could swim through the air. But it was no use. Their course was set now, and they wouldn't be able to stop or change direction until they made contact with the ceiling.

He looked down. It was a long way. The dead crop rows in the vegetable field looked like brown stripes. Bug looked like a gopher. Even Champion looked small from way up high, one of her rear legs braced against the pedestal of the control panel to keep herself from drifting away.

Lopside and Daisy continued to rise until Daisy's spine made contact with the top of the dome. A few seconds later, the top of Lopside's head clunked against it.

"We're here!" Daisy barked down to Champion. "We made it!"

"Good dogs," Champion called up.

They'd landed with the crack several yards behind them.

Daisy barked with pride, but not wanting to risk losing his bite on the nozzle, Lopside didn't even grunt in response. He just held his body still and rigid.

The next part of the mission was a delicate operation. Daisy used her tail and butt and muzzle to push gently against the dome and rotate so that her paws touched the ceiling. She'd have to keep just enough contact to be able to walk along and get over to the fissure. If she used too much force, she'd push off the ceiling and away.

"Here I go," Daisy said with confidence that Lopside didn't share.

Another screech of cracking glass almost launched Lopside's breakfast ERP into zero-gravity.

Daisy took step after careful step. She managed to get them close to the crack without losing contact with the dome, which was great. The problem was, even her lightest tread was enough to jar Lopside from his position. His body turned, and he ended up with his butt facing the crack.

Daisy cocked one of her rear legs and let Lopside have it in the rump. The kick was insulting, but it had its intended effect. Lopside spun around, and when his nose was pointed at the crack, Daisy kicked him again to stop him from rotating too far.

"I'm going to bite you now," Daisy said.

Lopside managed a warning growl, but Daisy ignored it. She clamped down on his haunch, hard. Her teeth didn't penetrate his flesh, but it still hurt.

As angry as it made Lopside, he understood that Daisy was just trying to hold him in place. Because once he squeezed the nozzle, the foam leaving the hose would act like a rocket engine and he'd be an out-of-control missile.

Lopside closed his jaws down on the nozzle's lever. Foam shot out with sudden force, propelling both Lopside and Daisy backward. A few wads of it landed on the fissure, but most of it went everywhere except for where Lopside wanted it to.

There was an awful screech that Lopside felt all the way down in his bones, and with sickening terror, he saw the fissure grow another inch. Even worse than the screech was a cold whisper. It was the unmistakable sound of air leakage. The fur on his face rippled in a distinct breeze. The crack was growing, air was escaping, and Lopside was pretty sure the entire dome would shatter.

He clamped down harder on the nozzle, squeezing the lever and firing emergency foam without any thought to direction or target. He just needed to get the foam out of the tank, all of it, right now.

His jaws ached and he whipped around on the end of the hose, but he held on.

The foam started coming out of the nozzle in sputters, and then stopped coming out entirely. The tank was empty. And with another shriek, the fissure expanded.

Daisy's nails scratched against the plasteel surface as she scrabbled for something—anything—to hold on to as suction drew them closer to the crack. But along with Daisy and Lopside, the escaping air pulled in wads and blobs of sprayed foam. Lopside had been counting on this. The foam started to clump over the crack, and each clump that made contact stuck there.

"Good dog," Daisy barked, realizing what Lopside had done.

More wads of foam drifted near them, and they batted them with paws and noses and tails to direct them over to the crack.

Eventually, the foam coated the fissure and began to harden in place.

The hiss of leaking air stopped.

The crack was sealed.

Lopside and Daisy shared silent, breathless grins. Daisy's slobbery tongue hung from her mouth in joy.

"The next time I get a biscuit, consider it yours," Lopside said.

"Okay! I'd offer to share it, but I'm really hungry."

"You know we don't actually have any biscuits? These are just imaginary biscuits."

"Then it's pretty stingy of you to only give me one."

Lopside could produce no argument against this accusation. "Prepare for landing," he barked.

Daisy coiled her body and thrust out her legs, pushing off from the dome.

They descended slowly, like balloons who'd lost most of their helium, and Lopside looked forward to a soft landing.

And then gravity took its hold again. Lopside felt like a

big paw was pressing his belly, and they crashed the last few feet to the deck.

Daisy broke his fall, and he lay on top of her for a while, catching his breath.

"Ouch," Daisy barked.

Bug came over and licked her nose. "Sorry. I think I mistimed turning the gravity back on."

"Ouch," Daisy agreed.

Glancing up at the repair, Lopside doubted the scum of dried emergency foam would be enough to save them. All they'd done was patch over another problem. Maybe the patch would last only a few hours or a few minutes. But right now, at this moment, the pack was still alive. Lopside laid his head on the deck and gave himself permission to be proud of that.

FOURTEEN

LOPSIDE IMAGINED SLEEPING NEXT TO a giant aquarium. And he imagined there was a crack in the glass. And the only thing repairing the crack was a smear of dried toothpaste. And swimming inside the tank was a pack of dog-eating sharks, venomous jellyfish, and electric eels. And the eels had laser eyes, because why not? Death and mayhem and laser eyes held at bay by nothing more than toothpaste.

Outside the dome, the star HD 24040 shone weakly like a speck of ash. The ship was still traveling from the momentum of the disastrous pulse engine firing, but the burn had been too short. Exactly how far they were from Stepping Stone, none of them knew. The agricultural dome was only equipped with short-range sensors, enough to scan the planet from orbit to find a safe landing spot, not reach out across billions of miles of empty space. Bug was working to increase their range, and all of them were working to maintain hope. It would take a miracle to reach the planet, and it was everyone's job to survive long enough to give a miracle a chance.

But they couldn't work around the clock. Their top priority was to make the dome's resources last as long as possible, and to make themselves last as long as possible. That meant enforced rest periods to conserve energy.

Daisy lay curled in the tightest ball she could make, her nose buried under her tail. "What are you most looking forward to about Stepping Stone?"

Bug was snuggled up beside Daisy. "I'm looking forward to cattle. I mean, I know we only have two cow embryos in the freezer, and two cows aren't really enough to count as a herd, but if they have babies, we'll have more cows. I want a hundred cows."

"That's a lot of cows," Daisy said.

Bug scoffed. "It's in my breeding. I can handle them. We corgis herd cattle by nipping their ankles to keep them in line, and I'm good at nipping ankles."

A wave of warm feelings for Bug passed through Lopside. They'd fought over shutting off the freezers barely more than a day ago, but it already seemed like a distant memory.

Lopside climbed up Daisy's back and curled atop her like the top layer of a cake. He rose and fell with her breaths. "What are you looking forward to, Daisy?"

"I want to run," she said. "Not like I do here, skidding a lot and bumping into things. I just want a big space where I can run and run and run, so far and so fast that I'm not even thinking anymore. Just running."

Lopside closed his eyes. He could picture it, her limbs carrying her over the ground like a galloping horse. He hoped she would have a chance to run on Stepping Stone. He hoped she would have a chance to grow out of her puppy awkwardness under a new sky.

"How about you, Champion?"

Lopside figured she'd say she was looking forward to fulfilling the mission. Or searching and rescuing. Something a pack leader would say. But Champion thumped her tail on the deck.

"I want to swim," she said.

Lopside snuffled, surprised. He hated water. Water

always washed good stink off him. The only good thing about being abandoned by Roro and the human crew was that he hadn't had to take a bath since before they went into hibernation.

"I'm a retriever," Champion went on. "I was bred to leap into water and swim. There's water on Stepping Stone, and I'm going to swim every day."

"It's too bad we have to ration water on the *Laika*," Bug said. "We could fill a tub for you."

Champion barked a small laugh. "Thanks, Bug. It wouldn't be the same."

She sighed, and Lopside could tell she was lost in thought.

"What are you looking forward to, Lopside?" she said after a long while.

Lopside didn't know what to say. Life on Stepping Stone wasn't supposed to be easy. They'd have to grow their own food. Sometimes there'd be cyclones and violent lightning storms. And there'd be plenty of unknown risks as well. But at least on Stepping Stone he wouldn't have to be scared of the sky cracking open and losing its atmosphere. He wouldn't always be hungry. He wouldn't always be cold. He'd be home.

"I just hope there'll be rats."

The pack fell silent. Lopside listened to their breathing and the small noises of the dome systems. He thought he was the only one awake when Daisy let out the tiniest whine.

"We're probably never going to get there, are we?"

No, probably not, Lopside thought.

But that was not what he said.

"We'll get there somehow. You're going to run, Daisy. And Bug is going to manage massive herds of livestock. And Champion's going to swim. We are going to be home. So we'd better be ready for landing."

Champion licked her paw. "That's right."

"That's right," Bug agreed.

"That's right," Daisy said with a happy lolling tongue.

"That's right," Lopside said.

FIFTEEN

WARNING: SINGULARITY CORE COLLAPSE IS *immi-*
nent. Warning: Singularity core collapse is imminent.

Lopside stood atop the control panel and stared at the
blinking red letters. Considering the dire message, the
alarm that woke him should have been screamed with a
great, dramatic clanging that left no doubt the *Laika* was
on the verge of utter destruction. Instead, it was just a small
beep, barely enough to annoy him out of slumber. The
other three dogs still snoozed and snored in a furry mound.

Maybe he was worrying too much. He didn't really
know how big an emergency this was, so calmly and qui-
etly, he jumped down from the control panel.

"Bug? Bug, wake up," he said, nudging the corgi with his nose. "I need to ask you something."

"Go 'way," Bug growled, taking a swipe at Lopside's face with his chubby paw.

"Okay, but just one question. How bad is 'Warning: singularity core collapse is imminent'?"

Bug's eyes bugged out. Still dizzy from sleep, he made a wobbly run to the control panel.

"So? Is it bad?"

"EVERYONE WAKE UP WE'RE GOING TO DIE!" Bug barked.

"So it's pretty bad."

Champion and Daisy jumped up as if their tails were on fire. They raced over to the control panel, and Bug filled them in: "That unstable singularity core in the Tesseract motor I was worried about? It must have finally failed, which means the entire engineering module is being flooded with anti-gravitons. Which means in a few minutes the *Laika* is going to explode."

"Please tell me there's good news," Champion said.

"That *was* the good news."

Lopside didn't want to hear the bad news, but Bug provided it anyway.

"If I'm wrong, instead of an anti-graviton explosion, the Tesseract motor is going to collapse in on itself, taking us and the entire ship with it, and we're all going to be crushed like—"

"Like a bug," Lopside finished for him.

"No. Smaller than a bug. Smaller than an atom. More like a single, eensy-weensy, almost-impossible-to-imagine point in space. A massive explosion is the *best-case* scenario."

Bug was panting with fear now, and Lopside's own breath quickened.

Champion licked her lips. "Options?"

The dogs stared at one another in silence. No one had an idea, and as the silence stretched, the desperation of their situation became even more clear.

"We can shelter in the garbage chute," Bug said finally.

That made no sense to Lopside. "If the *Laika* explodes or collapses, we're still dead in the garbage chutes."

"Yes," Bug agreed.

Lopside growled. "Then why did you suggest it?"

"The silence was killing me. Okay, what about using Rover Two as a lifepod?"

The Rover Lopside had taken out to redirect the communications dish was no longer in an accessible part of the ship, but Rover Two was in the secondary airlock attached to the dome.

But the Rover couldn't save them.

"I'm the only one who fits in the Rover," Lopside said.

"I know, but better one of us survives than none," Bug said.

Bug's go-down-with-the-ship statement was a harsh reminder that the human crew had done exactly the opposite. They'd abandoned the ship with the dogs still on board.

"I'm not leaving the ship without the pack." Lopside spread his legs, daring anyone to even try to move him.

"Affirmative," Champion said.

At least a full, precious minute had passed, and they were still no closer to a solution.

"Any ideas at all? Daisy?" Champion asked. If they were hoping for Daisy to come up with a good idea, then things were really desperate.

Daisy spit out her ball. "Isn't the dome designed to detach?"

It was, but not in a situation like this. The mission plan called for the *Laika* to establish orbit around Stepping Stone. Only then would the dome separate from the rest of the ship and use its descent thrusters to land softly on the surface of Stepping Stone. The dome's engines weren't designed for long-range travel.

But what other choice did they have?

They all looked at Champion, waiting for her decision. Lopside was glad he wasn't lead dog. He could see the weight of the impossible choice on Champion's face. He could smell her stress.

She focused her eyes on him. They were pleading.

"Make the decision," Lopside said. "We trust you."

She smelled of gratitude, and then she was fully Champion again. She gave the order with commanding authority: "Separate the dome."

The pack snapped into action.

Separating the dome required more than throwing a switch or two. It was a complicated process, and Lopside hoped he remembered his training.

Daisy volunteered her back as a ladder to help Lopside and Bug climb onto the control panel. Bug pressed multiple buttons, and Lopside hit a few more. "Releasing dome anchors," intoned a computerized voice.

A deep groan rumbled beneath the deck, followed by huge mechanical noises, the sounds of massive steel hooks that connected the dome to the rest of the ship. *KRUNK.*

CRONK. KRARK. WHEEZE. KRUNK.

"I didn't like that *cronk*," Champion said.

"The *cronk* is normal," Bug assured her. "I'd be worried if it didn't *cronk*. It's the *krark* that scares the tail off me."

Lopside and Bug continued to press buttons. The deck vibrated with a low hum that felt like an earthquake as the dome thrusters powered up. Then, a gigantic whirring sound as the thrusters swiveled in the direction Lopside had set them to.

"Thirty seconds," the computer said.

Lopside raised his paw to press the final button. He held it in midair.

Maybe the computer was wrong. Maybe the sensors had malfunctioned, and the *Laika* wasn't going to destruct after all. What was he doing? He was about to abandon the ship for a plasteel shelter with barely any engine power. With a single button, he could be killing his pack.

He brought his paw down on the button.

The computer said something, but he couldn't make out the words over the roar of the thrusters firing. Ordinarily, the thrusters would fire just enough to nudge the dome away from the *Laika*. In simulator training, it was just a gentle drifting sensation. But gentleness would kill them now. Lopside had set them to fire with full power.

The force was like the press of a giant hand. Lopside's lungs flattened, struggling to draw air. Everything in the dome shook. The dry crops crackled and crunched like brittle paper. Steel groaned. Neatly stored supplies tumbled off shelves.

With tooth-gnashing effort, Lopside forced himself to turn over on his back to look out the dome at the *Laika*. His eyes landed on the repaired crack. Flakes of emergency foam shook loose and fell like snow.

He watched the *Laika* recede as the dome pulled away. The ship didn't look so bad from here. Even the hole in the hull didn't look too big. It was hard to believe the ship was so badly damaged they'd had to leave it behind.

But it was.

There was a flash of silver-white light and an expanding plume of glitter, pinpoints smaller than stars.

Everything that the *Laika* was came apart in fragments—the engineering module, the command-and-control module, the crew quarters. The medical module and the hibernation chambers. The hull panels, the deck plates, the control panels. The gangways and tunnels where Lopside searched for rats. The chairs and tables in the galley where the crew shared meals. The bunks and the pillows and blankets where they slept. The beds and blankets and toys in the kennel, where Roro read them stories. All of that was gone. Now, it was just a collection of junk flying in all directions.

Because sound didn't travel through space, it happened in silence.

The dogs matched the silence, barkless and breathless, watching the loss of their ship.

And somehow, at that moment, Lopside forgave the humans. Not until he witnessed the destruction of the *Laika* did he understand how scared they must have been when they scurried into their lifepod and left the ship behind. They must have been desperate. They must have been sad.

Lopside let out one brief, mournful howl. It was not a howl for himself, but a howl for the humans.

Debris from the *Laika* chased the dome through space like a pack of angry squirrels. Just one screw, or a bread knife from the galley, could strike the dome and crack it wide open. Lopside urged the dome's thrusters to outrun them.

"How long will the thrusters keep firing?" Champion asked.

"Until they run out of fuel," Bug said.

"And how long is that?"

"I don't know. They're designed to land the dome on the planet, not fly through space. Another minute, maybe."

The dome shuddered and jangled. It wasn't going fast enough. The squirrels caught up, and Lopside flinched at every impact as small fragments of the *Laika* hit the dome.

It wasn't fair. He thought about all the things that had to happen for him to have arrived at this moment, in this place. He had to be adopted by the family with the man and the woman and the boy who smelled like chocolate milk. The man had to leave him by the tree in the park for Roro to jog by and find him. Lopside had to work hard and prove himself worthy of space travel.

He and the other dogs had trained so hard. They'd survived so much. But Lopside didn't think they'd survive this.

More debris struck the glass, leaving little white clusters of cracks.

"We're good dogs," Lopside said to his packmates.

Champion looked at him with soft, brown eyes. She understood he was saying good-bye. "Yes, we are all very good dogs."

"Even Daisy," Bug said.

"Even Bug," Daisy said.

They sniffed each other's butts and waited for the dome to shatter.

SIXTEEN

THE DOME DID NOT SHATTER, and for another day or another hour or another minute, the Barkonauts were still alive. That was their mission now: to survive as long as possible. If they failed to survive, nothing was possible. But if they succeeded . . . ?

To save power, they turned down the heat so low that their breaths frosted, and they dimmed the solar lamp to nighttime levels. They turned the gravity generators down to half.

That part wasn't so bad, actually. Lopside liked bouncing around the dome, jumping ten feet in the air and coming down for a soft landing. With a running start, Daisy could leap across the entire width of the dome in a single bound. Games of midair chase and tug-of-war helped keep their minds off the seriousness of the situation. Champion watched with longing, wanting to join in, but her leg needed more time to heal.

They continued to listen to stories they'd already heard many times over. They listened to the story of Jade, a German shepherd who rescued a human baby left inside a bag in the woods. And Chips, the war dog who charged into a machine gun nest to save his soldiers from being shot to pieces. And Smoky, a Yorkshire terrier who performed tricks for hospital patients and was considered by some to be the very first therapy dog.

"Do you think they'll tell stories about us someday?" Daisy said, snuggled with the others on their plastic tarp. Lopside lay curled up with the chicken eggs against his belly to keep them warm.

"No," Bug said. "Someday we'll tell our own stories."

Things were quiet for a while, the four dogs inside the cold dome, crawling through space, until Lopside said, "Play another story."

"I wish we could hear about Laika," Daisy said, maybe for the thousandth time.

Bug sighed. "Me, too. I keep trying to find the file

on Roro's tablet, but it's no use. It's like it's been erased or something."

It was still the only story in *The Great Book of Dogs* they hadn't heard.

Champion cleared her throat. "Listen, about the story of Laika—"

At that moment, Daisy let out a long, wailing howl. Startled, the other dogs leaped up and frantically sniffed her for injury or sickness.

"I'm okay," she said with a sadly thumping tail. "I just miss Roro, that's all."

Lopside's own tail drooped. "We all do, Daisy."

They sniffed her again and resettled into their heap.

Lopside gave Champion an extra sniff. She was giving off a strange scent. "What was that you were saying about Laika?"

Champion rested her chin on her paws. "Nothing," she said. "Nothing."

Bip–bip–bip.

Beep–beep–beep.

Bip–bip–bip.

The electronic tones had come from the communications panel.

"Did I just imagine that?" Lopside asked, not daring to believe.

"No," Champion said, her voice gruff. "I heard it, too."

Lopside raced to the panel, the three other dogs trailing him.

They stood in a near silence of held breaths and strong heartbeats. They strained to listen, waiting, hoping the sounds would repeat.

Bip-bip-bip.

Beep-beep-beep.

Bip-bip-bip.

There was no mistaking it.

Three bips, three beeps, three bips.

Three dots, three dashes, three dots.

"Morse code," said Lopside. "SOS."

Someone was out there in the dark of space.

And they were calling for help.

SEVENTEEN

THE PACK TOOK TURNS KEEPING watch over the control panel in case another SOS signal came through. But none did. Maybe the sensors had malfunctioned. Maybe they'd picked up some random bit of radiation bouncing around the asteroids. But Lopside couldn't let it go. It was Morse code. He was sure of it. And that meant there were survivors out there. And if there were survivors, they had to be the *Laika*'s crew, because who else so far from Earth would know to send out a distress signal in Morse code?

"Even if they survived, how would we find them?" Bug argued. "Space is endlessly dark and vast. This is worse than looking for a needle in a haystack. This is like looking for a black needle in a black haystack taller than you can imagine."

Daisy cocked her head in confusion. "What's hay got to do with it?"

"He's saying we're looking for a lifepod in space," Champion cut in. "A tiny lifepod. In huge space."

Lopside didn't want to hear anything more about needles and hay. He leaped in the reduced gravity and made it easily to the top of the sensor control panel.

On the left side of the display screen glowed a green ball labeled *Laika Agricultural Dome*. In the center of the screen was a white dot labeled HD 24040—the distant star. A number of smaller dots orbited the star, and one of them was labeled Stepping Stone. Dozens of more dots and squares and triangles represented moons and comets and asteroids. He lifted his head and looked out the dome. The nearest objects, a cluster of asteroids, were too far away and too small and too dim to see with the naked eye. On the sensor screen they showed up as tiny red triangles, not much more than freckles.

The Morse signal returned: *bip-bip-bip, beep-beep-beep, bip-bip-bip.*

The same sequence now, over and over.

"That settles it," Lopside said.

Champion stood on her hind legs and rested her paws on the control panel. She panted with the pain from putting weight on her broken leg, but didn't complain.

"The signal has to be coming from the asteroid field," Lopside said, putting his paw over the little red triangles. "It's only three hundred miles away."

Champion regarded the display for a long time. "I don't see what difference it makes. Three hundred miles or three hundred million miles. We have no engine capability. We couldn't get closer to the asteroids even if we wanted to. Instead of wasting our time on the impossible, we should work on rigging up a transmitter. If we could get a signal out to whoever's sending the SOS—"

Daisy lay on her belly and covered her eyes with her paws as Champion and Bug started arguing about what to do next.

Lopside barely listened to them. He stared at the display. The dome was just a few hours away from the asteroids. Compared to most distances in space, it was almost nothing, barely more than one small step. Bobbie the Wonder Dog had walked on his own for months. He'd crossed an impossible distance and faced dangers and hardships, all in the hope of finding his family again.

Lopside made a decision.

"The Rover," he said.

Champion and Bug swallowed their barks. Daisy peered at Lopside through her paws. He had their attention.

"The Rover can do it. Just a few puffs from the maneuvering jets and it'll go and keep on going until acted upon by another force. That's Newton's First Law, right?"

"Yes," conceded Bug. "The same reason the dome is drifting toward Stepping Stone. Once on course, it'll keep going unless something pulls it off course. But as slow as we're going we'll be long dead by the time we make it to the planet."

"But I'm not talking about the planet," Lopside argued. "I'm just talking about getting the Rover to the asteroid field. I'm talking about looking for survivors."

Lopside could tell Champion was about to come up with reasons why he couldn't do it, so he interrupted her before she could open her muzzle.

"With a fresh air recycler unit and a few ERPs, a dog could last for days inside the Rover."

"Let's say you survived in the Rover long enough to get to the nearest asteroid," Champion said. "Look at the display, Lopside. There are *hundreds* of asteroids, spread out across thousands of miles. It's still a needle in a haystack, and making it out to the haystack is going to kill you."

"It's a lot to risk," Bug said. "Too much."

Lopside barked. "It's what Barry the Saint Bernard would do, heading out in a blizzard to save lost skiers. It's what Balto and Togo would do to bring medicine across frozen tundra."

"Those are stories," Champion said. "For every Barry who became a hero, there are dozens of dogs who got lost in a blizzard and never came back. Even dogs whose owners left them out in the snow to freeze to death."

The pack was against Lopside. He supposed it didn't matter. He wasn't like the rest of them. He wasn't bred with an instinct to please others. His instinct was to go out on his own. He could wait till they were asleep and then sneak out to the secondary airlock and take the Rover without telling them.

But he wasn't just a dog.

He was a space dog.

A Barkonaut.

And the humans weren't just crewmates. They were pack.

"I wouldn't be risking myself to save just any humans," Lopside said. "I'd be risking it to save Commander Lin. And Crew Specialist Dimka. And Medical Officer Ortega."

He could smell Champion's resolve begin to waver.

"I'd be risking my life for Roro."

He wagged his tail.

Even though the prospect of leaving the pack and the dome behind and setting out into the unknown terrified him, he couldn't help but be excited. The human crew was somewhere out there. Roro was out there. He believed it. He *knew* it. Almost.

Gingerly, Champion lowered herself to the ground. "Do you want to hear Laika's story?" she said.

Lopside jumped down off the control panel. "But . . . it's not in the book."

"I know it's not," Champion said. "I listened to it. And then I erased it."

At first Lopside could only stare, dumbfounded. Then, slowly, like a kettle coming to a boil, he felt pressure building in his head. Resentment. Anger. Fury. Glaring hard into Champion's brown eyes, he said, "You are a bad dog."

Bug looked like he wanted to bite her. Even Daisy vibrated with a low, dangerous growl.

Champion's tail drooped. "I know I'm a bad dog," she said. "And I'm sorry. I thought . . . if you and the others knew Laika's story . . . her full story . . . it would change things. It would change the way you feel."

"About you?" Lopside didn't know how his feelings for Champion right now could change for the worse.

"No. About humans. About Roro."

How could Laika's story change the way he felt about Roro? How could his feelings change for the person who had found him in the cold mud next to a tree on a rainy morning?

"Do you want to hear it now?"

Lopside hesitated. Champion wasn't acting superior. She was frightened, and not for herself. He sensed that more was at stake than just his curiosity.

"Yes," Lopside said. "I want to hear it. I want to hear it now."

"We all do," Bug said.

"Then come with me," Champion said, limping away. "We'll meet at the tarp."

EIGHTEEN

"**LAIKA WAS A STRAY LIVING** in the streets of Moscow in the 1950s. It wasn't the worst place for a dog. People liked dogs there. They didn't treat them like vermin to be chased off and killed. Instead, they accepted them as part of city life. They let strays sleep in doorways, or the lobbies of buildings. Dogs had free run of the subways. They could get on the trains and ride them wherever they wanted to. But it still must have been a tough life for Laika. Moscow in winter is terribly cold."

Nobody lay down or curled up on the plastic tarp as Champion told the story. All the dogs sat straight on their haunches. Champion hadn't chosen this place because it was cozy and comforting, but because the place where the dogs slept was an important place, and the story of Laika was important.

"She must have thought she was lucky to be chosen by the Soviet space program," Champion went on. "She was out of the weather, indoors, and warm. They gave her the best food. They made sure she was healthy. She was never alone, never lonely. She had all kinds of visitors. Important people, photographers, reporters. They were delighted at everything she did. She would chew on a bone and they would laugh. She would chase a ball and they'd applaud. She had no way of knowing that it would all come to an end. When the engineers sealed her inside her spaceship, a little steel ball they called Sputnik 2, she must have thought she'd be seeing their smiling faces again soon. But it was never their plan to bring Laika home alive. They knew she would die in space. The engineers, the technicians, the reporters, even the public. Everyone knew it. Everyone except Laika."

Lopside thought the gravity had failed, because the floor seemed to tilt sideways, and his stomach seemed to float up into his throat. But it wasn't a mechanical problem.

It was the realization of what Champion had just told them.

"Laika was supposed to run out of oxygen and suffocate painlessly. Instead, there was a malfunction, and she overheated. Honestly, I don't know if it matters how she died. All I know is she went up there not knowing the truth about her own mission, and she died alone. Proving they had the technology to send a living dog into space was more important to her masters than bringing her back alive. And our trainers back on Earth knew this whole story. Our ship's human crew knew it. Commander Lin knew it." She paused and looked into Lopside's eyes. "And Roro knew it, too."

None of the dogs said anything for a while. Daisy let out a small whimper, but that was it.

"Do you believe me?" Champion said at last.

"Yes," Daisy said miserably.

Bug grunted. "Yes."

They all looked at Lopside, waiting to hear what he'd say.

He was angry at Champion, but he knew she was telling the truth.

"Then I'm going to ask you again," Champion said.

"Somewhere in that asteroid wilderness, there may be surviving members of our crew. And that's a big maybe. That SOS could be a stray signal, bouncing around space. It could be coming from a piece of lifepod wreckage. It could be anything. But if it is a survivor, it's a human from a ship named after a brave dog who was lied to. Who was blasted into space without knowing it was a one-way trip, that she was being sent up to die. Do you still want to risk your life for that, Lopside?"

The answer froze in Lopside's throat.

What was the last thing Laika saw before being sealed into her capsule?

It must have been a human.

Did the human pet her? Did the human scritch her?

Did Laika get a final belly rub? Did anyone sneak her a last treat?

Did she get a smile?

Did anyone tell her she was a good dog?

Did she feel loved?

If the answer to any of those questions was yes, that only made it worse. It meant that humans could give comfort and affection and love while telling a lie. They could call you a good dog while sending you to your death.

Knowing that truth, how could Lopside still be loyal to a human?

"Are we even Barkonauts anymore?" He honestly wasn't sure.

"I think...yes," Bug said. "I think I'm still a Barkonaut."

"I don't know what else I'd be," Daisy said.

Champion sniffed Lopside's face. "I know what you're feeling," she said. "I asked myself the same questions. It's for each one of us to decide for themselves. But yes, I'm still a Barkonaut."

Hearing the others' answers helped Lopside form his own decision. Barkonauts were dogs who completed their missions. And that was what Lopside wanted to do.

"If there's someone to be saved," he said, "I'm going to try to save them."

Champion hesitated only a moment. "Then let's get to work."

NINETEEN

"YOU HAVE THREE ERPS, A fresh oxygen recycler, and a quart of almost fresh water," Bug told Lopside. "Okay, not very fresh at all, but it's drinkable."

The mood in the airlock smelled urgent and tense. Champion insisted that the Rover be checked, double-checked, triple-checked, and then checked again. Lopside was already exhausted and he hadn't even left the dome yet.

"How much propellant does the Rover have?" he asked.

"Half a gallon. That's enough for an hour of continuous fire. So don't waste it. Short squirts only. That's all you need to get moving or change direction. Momentum will do the rest."

"Newton's First Law," Lopside said, grateful for Bug's coaching. "I remember."

Daisy rushed up and shoved her big wet nose in Lopside's face. "It's not fair that I'm too big to fit in the Rover. You already went out once, and I haven't gotten to go out at all."

"I'm sorry," Lopside said. "You'll have to keep Bug and Champion safe while I'm gone."

Lopside touched his nose to hers, and somehow that small gesture felt as though he were saying good-bye, and he felt the weight of a million gravities.

Champion came over and sniffed his butt and muzzle to make sure he was okay. "Bug set the dome's comm system to send out a signal pulse once every thirty seconds. It'll sync with the Rover's comm, so that way we can keep track of your location."

The idea of keeping in contact with his packmates sent a wave of comfort spreading through Lopside's belly.

"Unless an asteroid interferes with your signal," Bug said. "Then we won't be able to talk and will have no idea where you are."

Bug was just a dog-shaped bucket of ice water.

Lopside wanted to get under way before he could

change his mind. "I'm ready. The Rover is more than ready. Let's get going."

And so he crawled into the Rover's tool compartment. Champion quadruple-checked to make sure Lopside was sealed in there good and tight, and then she, Daisy, and Bug squeezed into the tiny observation chamber outside the airlock.

"Comm check," Champion said over the radio. "Am I coming in?"

"Loud and clear," Lopside responded. He had to respond six more times before Champion was satisfied that the communications system was working.

"I'll be monitoring you every step of the way, no matter how long it takes," she said.

"*We'll* be monitoring," Bug cut in.

"If you don't open the airlock and let me outside right now I'm turning my radio off," Lopside threatened. He fooled nobody, including himself. He was scared. He wanted to stay inside the dome. He wanted to be with his pack. But if there were human survivors out among the asteroids, they must be even more scared.

"Opening airlock doors now," Champion said.

The double doors creaked open, and all the air in the

airlock escaped with a great whoosh.

"Lopside, report," Champion demanded.

"I'm fine. Release the clamps."

A small part of him hoped there'd be a malfunction and that the clamps wouldn't release and that Bug or Champion or even Daisy would come up with a brilliant, last-minute search-and-rescue plan that didn't involve Lopside venturing out all by himself in a fragile metal box. But he heard the now-familiar *ka-clunk* of the clamps releasing.

He leaned forward and nudged the maneuvering control with his nose. The tiny nozzle on the back of the Rover hissed, and the Rover floated out of the airlock, into the endless well of inky black.

Bug guided Lopside through a couple of maneuvers that involved brief firings of the nozzles until he was turned in the direction of the asteroid field. He couldn't make out any asteroids by naked eye. It was too dark, the asteroids too far away.

Maybe the sensors were wrong. Maybe the reason he couldn't see anything out there was because nothing *was* out there. But then he caught a brief glimmer, a distant rock catching a reflection off the even more distant sun.

Champion made him report in to make sure he wasn't

suffocating or overheating in the Rover, and then there was nothing left to do but give the nozzles a long burst to send him out, away from the dome.

Lopside gnawed on a particularly stale ERP. He wondered if Bug had gone out of his way to equip the Rover with the stalest ERPs he could find. If so, it was a smart move, because it let Lopside pass time by stubbornly chewing. He also entertained himself with ERP burps. In fact, a couple of hours into the journey, he burped out a song about Daisy.

Was he the first dog ever to musically burp in space?

Champion would have thought it odd and maybe even bad to be burping during a mission of such importance. But eating and burping and playing and working—these were the things he missed about daily life on the *Laika*, being with Roro and the rest of the crew, without every second of every minute being about surviving or enduring cold and hunger and eking a few more hours from the feeble batteries.

If only he could find human survivors, then they'd figure out a way to get the dome to Stepping Stone.

Humans and dogs, together.

🐾 🐾 🐾

After a lot of eating, burping, thinking, and a million check-ins with Champion, Lopside neared the asteroid field.

What had been nothing more than tiny triangles on a display screen were now tumbling boulders and small mountains. Some were sharp-edged and glittered with bright flecks of mineral. Some were lumpy masses of rock that looked like colossal potatoes, pitted with craters.

Lopside gave the Rover a few propellant bursts to match the asteroids' velocity and looked back toward the dome. He couldn't see any trace of it. It was too distant, its lights too dim. Lopside had never been so far away from another living creature.

To keep himself from panicking, he thought about Bobbie the Wonder Dog, who'd crossed 2,500 miles to find his family. Alone in the desert, or high in the mountains, maybe Bobbie had been even farther from humans and other dogs than Lopside was now. And he'd come out of it all right.

Lopside the Wonder Dog.

He liked how that sounded.

An object drifted by. Narrow and about a foot long, it didn't look like a hunk of rock. It looked human-made. Lopside gave the Rover a quick burst and entered a cloud of small, glittering bits of metal. Most of them were just fragments of something unidentifiable, but there were also screws and rivets and nuts. There was a torn and fluffy thing that looked like seat padding.

He knew what he was looking at. But it was the unthinkable. He held out hope it was something else until a larger piece almost hit the Rover. It was a metal plate with a few painted letters on it. Lopside made out an *L*, and an *I*, and an *F*, and an *E*.

LIFE.

There was only one thing it could be.

He swallowed and activated the radio. "This is Lopside," he said. "I've found the lifepod."

A crackle, and then Champion's voice: "Report lifepod's condition."

Lopside didn't want to answer. Because once he barked the words, once he heard them in his own head, it would be true, and he didn't want it to be true.

"Lopside? Report."

"It's in pieces," Lopside said. "The lifepod is in pieces. It's been destroyed."

TWENTY

A FULL MINUTE WENT BY without anyone saying anything over the radio. Lopside imagined his packmates back at the dome, silenced by disappointment, wondering what to do now. Lopside himself was just numb. He'd expected to find survivors. He'd expected to save them.

Dogs and humans, together.

Lopside and Roro, together.

His hopes, like the lifepod, were smashed into chunks and crumbs.

Champion's voice came on the radio. "See if there's anything to salvage. Engine parts, supplies, anything we can use."

Lopside tried to bark. Only a whimper came out. He

swallowed his grief and tried again. "Affirmative," he managed.

He turned his attention to the debris field. Most of it was just tiny bits the size of kibble pieces. Here and there he spotted a length of torn hosing, or a random fragment of metal. He doubted even Bug could find a use for any of it. But then he set eyes on a simple gray capsule the size and shape of a watermelon.

He gave the Rover a squirt and zipped close to it.

Was it . . . ?

"*Laika* dome, come in."

"Rover, this is *Laika* dome," Champion's bark answered.

"I've found the lifepod's singularity core containment unit."

When he heard back from the dome, it was Bug. "Do you see anything that looks like an anti-graviton generator?"

Lopside knew what Bug was thinking. A singularity core and an anti-graviton generator were the two components of a Tesseract motor. Under normal circumstances they wouldn't dream of using a Tesseract motor within a planetary system so close to gravitational fields. But these weren't ordinary circumstances. If there was the smallest, itty-bittiest chance of using the motor to warp space and shorten the distance between the dome and Stepping Stone, it might be worth it.

But it was pointless to think about. An anti-graviton generator would be as large as a refrigerator, and there was nothing even close to that size in sight.

"Negative on anti-graviton generator," Lopside said.

"Even a functioning singularity core is no use without anything to generate and control anti-gravitons. But you might as well grab the containment unit. Better than returning with empty paws." Lopside could hear the disappointment in Bug's barks.

Champion replaced Bug on the radio. "There's nothing else you can do out there, Lopside. Grab the unit, turn around, and come back to the dome," she ordered.

"Affirmative."

Lopside reached out with one of the Rover's arms and closed its claw around the capsule. He was leaning for the maneuver control when a bright, sharp sound filled the Rover's compartment.

Bip-bip-bip. Beep-beep-beep. Bip-bip-bip.

"*Laika* dome, come in!" Lopside barked, trying not to pant with excitement. "Did you hear that?"

Again: *Bip-bip-bip. Beep-beep-beep. Bip-bip-bip.*

"*Laika* dome, this is Rover, come in."

Lopside waited for a response from the dome. Seconds ticked by, and none came.

"Champion, this is Lopside, do you read me?"

When there was still no answer, Lopside looked back in the direction of the dome. A great whale of rock slowly drifted across his view. The asteroid must be blocking the dome's radio signal. It was probably blocking Lopside's, too. And maybe that was why the SOS signal only came in sporadic bursts. If an asteroid crossed the path of whoever or whatever was sending it, then the radio signal would be blocked until the asteroid was clear.

And this one was a huge asteroid, longer than the *Laika*, and slow as a cloud on a still day.

Lopside knew his signal wouldn't go through, but he felt he had to at least try: "Come in, *Laika* dome. Champion? Bug? Daisy?"

Just as he predicted, his radioed barks went out into the void without answer.

Had Bobbie the Wonder Dog had a radio?

No, he had not.

Lopside would have to do without.

The SOS signal, however, continued to blare.

Lopside knew he ought to wait until the big asteroid passed and then head back to the dome. Instead, he gave the Rover a burst and went deeper into the asteroid field.

The field grew thicker. He was in the shadows of giants, a mouse among elephants. If he ran into trouble out here, his pack would never find out what had happened to him.

"Focus on the mission," he scolded himself.

He was searching for anything that didn't look like the rough rock and metal of an asteroid. A piece of lifepod wreckage. Maybe even a piece of the lifepod that humans could survive in, like the crew compartment. He wished he could use his nose in space, because if he could, he knew he'd be able to sniff out a human.

Massive boulders tumbled lazily all around him. One was coming awfully close, and right before he took his eyes off it, he caught a flash of light.

Probably just a reflection of starlight off some shiny bit of material on the asteroid's surface.

Nothing to get excited about.

But if that was true, why was his tail thumping against the sides of the compartment?

The asteroid was still rolling, and the area from where the flash had originated passed out of view.

Lopside tried to contact the dome by radio again, but there was still no answer.

The SOS was louder than ever.

"This is Lopside of the Earth ship *Laika*. Do you read?" This time he wasn't trying to reach Champion at the dome. He was trying to reach the source of the SOS.

Still, nothing.

Maybe whoever was sending out the SOS had a transmitter, but not a receiver.

Maybe he was hearing a distress call sent out automatically by a piece of the lifepod's emergency system, and there was no one and nothing left to rescue but another smashed piece of space junk.

Maybe whoever was putting out the signal couldn't respond.

Maybe there was no one alive left to respond.

Lopside spun the Rover around and gave it a burst to catch up to the asteroid.

It loomed below him, at least a few miles across. As he brought the Rover closer to its surface, he could make out the detail of its terrain. He hovered several hundred feet above deep craters, their bottoms hidden in darkness. Valleys cut through the rock, with cliffs and ridges.

He descended and began skimming over the surface from a few dozen feet above. The Rover's work lamp cast a spotlight but didn't catch a sign of anything human-made, not even wreckage.

Then, a flash.

Lopside guided the Rover into the crater. The rim rose above him like the lips of a giant stone mouth. He followed the slope of the crater down, toward its floor, keeping his eyes fixed on the flashing light. If it was coming from life-pod wreckage, or even just a piece big enough to shelter the crew, surely he would have spotted it by now. But there was only the pulsating light and the insistent bips and beeps of the SOS.

He kept the Rover moving at a slow pace, his eyes darting over a landscape littered with rocks ranging from pebbles to slabs five times the size of Daisy.

There it was, the source of the light. A scuffed and dented cylinder about the size of a coffee cup. The light it gave off wasn't particularly bright. He'd imagined a great bonfire, a flaming tower, blasting the location of survivors like a rocket engine. But this was just a lone emergency beacon.

Lopside activated one of the Rover's arms. He reached

out with it and switched off the beacon. The light died, and the SOS fell silent.

It took a few seconds for his eyes to adjust to the darkness. And once they did, he saw it: At the foot of a boulder, almost completely buried in gravel, was a space suit glove. He stared at it a moment, not quite believing his eyes.

With the gentlest burst, he brought the Rover just inches above the glove and started scraping the gravel away with the claw. The asteroid had almost no gravity, and with every scrape pebbles and dust floated up to form a cloud. He didn't want to obscure his vision, so he dug slowly, deliberately.

The forearm of a long-term survival space suit emerged. Then the chest plate. Stenciled on it was the name *Laika*.

A whimper built up inside Lopside's throat, and he barely held it back.

Back in the dome, Champion had given Lopside tips on search-and-rescue operations. There was rescue, which was saving a living person. And there was recovery, which meant bringing back a corpse.

Lopside kept on with the grim business of unburying the suit.

When he excavated the helmet, he began to hope. Hope

was a mistake. He didn't want to hope, because there was very little reason for it. But he couldn't help it. His tail thwacked against the sides of the Rover's compartment. His ears stood at attention, even the floppy one. Maybe hope was his instinct.

He gingerly scraped away at the gravel and dust covering the helmet's faceplate. The dust formed a fine coat, and the claw was too crude a tool to do a good job of clearing it off. The very last thing he wanted to do was put a crack in it.

Finally, a face began to emerge. A human face. He couldn't make it out in the dimness of the crater. With a numb paw, he directed Rover's work lamp into the helmet.

The face was thin, the lips dried and cracked. A layer of frost covered the eyelids and cheeks.

It was her.

It was Roro.

TWENTY-ONE

LOPSIDE'S HOWL OF SADNESS ECHOED in the Rover's compartment, but he was the only one who could hear it.

He let himself keen for a total of six seconds. Six seconds to get it out of his system and clear his head so he could return to work.

Of all the outcomes he'd feared, this was the worst. Roro, dead. Roro, who'd rescued him from beneath a tree. Roro, who'd given him a bath to wash the mud out of his coat (which he hadn't enjoyed), but then had wrapped him in a thick, warm towel. Roro, who'd let him sleep on her bed. Roro, who'd convinced Space Operations that

Lopside was smart enough and determined enough to be trained for space.

He owed Roro everything. Humans and dogs, always together, and she was his human, and he was her dog.

Six seconds was all he gave himself to howl in pain.

There was still a job to do, and he was still a Barkonaut.

He continued digging to expose more of Roro's suit. There was a loop on the top of the life-support pack, and Lopside closed the Rover's claw around it. He was about to give the Rover a burst to start lifting Roro out of the crater when her fingers flexed.

"No," he told himself. He'd just imagined it. Or he'd accidentally shifted her suit and caused the movement himself.

Her fingers flexed again.

"Roro?" he barked. "Roro, it's me, Lopside!"

There was no answer. Not at first. But then Roro's eyelids twitched. Tiny flecks of frost fell away from her eyelashes, and she opened her brown eyes and stared directly into Lopside's.

They were the most miraculous eyes Lopside had ever seen, because they belonged to Roro, and she was alive.

Her weak voice crackled over the Rover's radio. "I'm dreaming."

"No, you're not. It's me, Lopside. And I'm here to rescue you."

Not recover. Rescue. He had no idea how she'd gotten here, how she was still alive. But those answers would wait. Right now, the only thing that mattered was getting her back to the dome.

"What's your condition?" he asked her, the way Champion would, making a question sound like an order.

She didn't answer. Maybe she was too weak to answer. But then Lopside remembered she wouldn't be able to, even if she'd been strong and healthy. All she could hear over the radio were barks. With him inside the Rover, she couldn't see his body language. She couldn't see his posture, or the angle of his ears, or the action of his tail, so her translation chip couldn't convert his dog communication into human language.

Solve the problem, Lopside thought to himself.

Then, to Roro, he barked: "Bark-bark-bark. Woof-woof-woof. Bark-bark-bark."

It was the shortest, simplest message he could think of.

Her eyes snapped fully open.

"Morse code? Oh, you clever dog."

"Report condition," he asked her again, this time barking in code.

"Weak. Cold." Her voice was a whisper.

"Report condition of survival suit."

She closed her eyes and didn't respond.

"Roro!" he barked as loud as he could. Roro's eyes popped back open, startled awake. "Report condition of survival suit," he code-barked again.

"Functional, but battery's at two percent."

That would explain why she was cold. Her suit was designed for survival, but even under the best conditions, it could only keep a human alive for two days, maybe three. Who knew how long she'd been in her suit, buried under gravel on the asteroid. Eventually, her oxygen recycler would fail, too, and then Lopside's mission would be a recovery job for sure.

He checked his own battery power. The Rover was down to thirty percent. That was enough to get him back to the dome, but not if he also used his battery to power Roro's suit.

He didn't see any other choice.

"How are the other dogs?" Roro asked. It sounded like she was having a hard time moving her lips.

"Soon," he code-barked. He hoped she understood he meant that she'd see them soon. Every message took a long time to bark, and he didn't want to waste time or breath.

The battery compartment on Roro's space suit was a box half the size of a loaf of bread, attached to her hip. Nosing the claw arm controls, he pried the cover off Roro's battery pack, exposing a black brick attached to cables: her suit battery.

Next, he extended the claw arm to its full length. His own battery pack was on the back side of the Rover. He couldn't even see it from inside the tool compartment. After too much fumbling, he gave up the delicate approach and just knocked the claw against the case lid: *klunk, klunk, klunk*. He didn't know he'd popped the lid off until he saw it float away.

He gave the Rover a burst to spin it around so the exposed battery compartment faced Roro.

"Plug," he code-barked.

He had to bark it three more times before Roro understood what he was telling her to do.

Slowly, sluggishly, she disconnected the power line from

her own battery and plugged it into the Rover's battery.

"Heater working?" he code-barked.

"Yes," Roro said. "I can feel it." He could hear the relief in her voice.

Lopside hooked the claw through the loop on the back of Roro's suit. He told her to hold still and get ready, and with a good, strong burst of propellant, they lifted off from the crater, into a black sky filled with a tumult of asteroids.

All he had to do was drag Roro back to the dome.

Assuming he could even find the dome again.

And avoid collisions with asteroids.

And do it while sharing precious battery power.

"Lopside, if your battery drops below fifty percent, unhook me." Her voice was still weak and whispery. She was spending a lot of effort to get all the words out.

Lopside didn't tell her his battery was already down to thirty percent. Maybe disobeying her made him a bad dog. But he hadn't come all this way just to abandon her.

"Pack members stay together," he barked back at Roro.

She said nothing. Maybe she'd fallen asleep or unconscious.

He gave the Rover another burst and set out into the wide open.

TWENTY-TWO

LOPSIDE AIMED TOWARD THE GREAT, whale-shaped asteroid drifting between him and the dome.

He hadn't had contact with his pack in hours. It was just him in the Rover, dragging Roro with one claw arm and the lifepod's singularity core containment unit with another. The slender battery cable drained power from the Rover and fed it to Roro's suit.

Roro wasn't saying much.

Lopside would ask her condition in barked Morse code, and she would mumble something he couldn't make out.

He didn't think it was a technical issue. Judging by the Rover's battery meter, her suit was getting enough power to keep her environmental controls operating. She should be warm enough in there.

By contrast, giving the Rover's power to her suit meant that Lopside was getting colder. His paw pads ached, and his breath fogged the tool compartment's windows.

"Keep a steady course," he told himself. Eventually the whale asteroid would pass and then he'd be able to contact the dome again.

All he had to do was keep going for the whale.

And stay awake.

The colder he got, the harder that was.

"Roro," he code-barked. "Story. Tell."

"Story?" she croaked.

"Affirmative. Tell me story. About dog."

He wanted to keep Roro conscious and talking so she didn't slip away and never come back. He wanted to keep his mind occupied on something other than the cold and the distance. And he needed courage.

"Please," he code-barked.

After nothing but silence, Lopside thought Roro had lost consciousness. But then, "There was a small dog," she began. Her voice sounded so far away that Lopside looked behind him to make sure she was still attached to the Rover.

"A small dog who only knew his past and his present. And neither of those were very good. A family who didn't take care of him. A tree to stand next to in a rainstorm."

Lopside had an idea where this story was going, but he didn't interrupt. He wanted to hear it.

"You should have seen him," Roro went on. "All drooped over, his ears limp, a mess of wet fuzz. So sad and so adorable. He was scared and cold and miserable. But not broken. He had spirit. He had hope. All he needed was warmth and food and love. All he needed was a chance for a future that he could have never imagined. Most of the people at Space Operations didn't see why anyone would recruit him for the Barkonauts program. He was too small. Too rough. Not a purebred. But one person knew better. She knew all he needed was a chance to learn and train with some of the best dogs in the world. A chance to travel into space. To travel faster and farther than any dog in the whole history of dogs. A chance to prove how strong he was, by surviving catastrophe after catastrophe. A chance to show how brave he was, by venturing into an asteroid field and rescuing one silly human being."

Despite the bone-crushing chill in the Rover, Lopside felt warm. Or maybe not warm. It was too cold to even imagine warmth. But there was light. It was just a tiny pinpoint, like a distant star that held out promise. He needed to hold on to that spark.

He had to be the best dog he could be.

Like Bobbie, who walked longer and farther than should have been possible.

Like Barry, the Saint Bernard who brought hikers back from avalanches.

Like Bug, the stubbornest dog he'd ever met.

Like Champion, who'd risked her life to drag food into the dome so the pack wouldn't starve.

Like Daisy, who basically just rolled around on the floor a lot but could make a splint with her strong teeth and jaws.

Like Lopside, who would not let Roro die.

He had to be a good dog.

TWENTY-THREE

LOPSIDE WAS ONLY HALF-AWAKE WHEN he heard someone barking in his ear.

He shook his sluggish head.

"Rover, this is *Laika* dome. Do you read?"

A pause.

"Lopside, this is Champion. Do you read?"

Her barking sounded both urgent and exhausted at the same time. How long had Lopside been asleep? How long had Champion been calling for him?

"Dome. I read you."

Celebratory barks and yips over the radio filled the Rover's compartment. He also heard Champion's sharp bark telling Bug and Daisy to shut up.

"What's your condition, Lopside?"

Good question. He could see nothing out of the Rover's window, just the damp film of his own breath. His battery was down to less than three percent. And he only had enough propellant for one or two more bursts. But that wasn't his biggest concern.

"Roro?" he barked.

"Mmm?"

Good. At least she was still alive.

Lopside reported everything to Champion. Then he asked, "How far off course am I?"

It was Bug who answered: "You're pointed the wrong way, but you're only about one-third of a mile outside the secondary airlock. Bobbie the Wonder Dog couldn't have done better. Stand by for directions."

Bug instructed Lopside to give the Rover a tiny burst to rotate it so that when he gave the final burst, one that would use up the very last of the Rover's propellant, he would glide into the airlock.

If Lopside made a mistake, or Bug made a mistake, he would sail right past the dome, and he would keep going, and there would be nothing left to do but bark some long good-byes as his battery drained to nothing and he and

Roro froze to death.

But he discovered he wasn't afraid.

He wouldn't make a mistake.

Neither would Bug.

He trusted himself, and he trusted his pack.

Stretching his neck, he brought his nose right up to the nozzle control.

"Okay," Bug said. "You're good. Pull the trigger."

"Affirmative," Lopside said. "We're coming home."

TWENTY-FOUR

LOPSIDE AND RORO WERE GREETED by invasive sniffs and lapping tongues and wagging tails and out-of-control yips and barks and panting. Roro removed her helmet, moving her arms slowly, as if they weighed a hundred pounds each, and though tears fell from her half-closed eyes, she smiled.

"My dogs," she said over and over. "My good, good dogs."

They had a million questions for her.

What had happened to the lifepod?

Where was the rest of the crew?

How had she survived, and how long had she spent on the surface of the asteroid?

But it was Daisy who put a stop to it.

"She needs rest," she barked, and the way she said it left no room for argument. Letting Roro lean on her, Daisy led her away from the airlock and told her to lie down on the Barkonauts' tarp.

While Daisy brought Roro a mix of water, ERPs, and electrolytes from the medical supplies, Champion nudged Lopside away. When they were far enough from the pack that they could talk in private, Champion said, "We need to know."

Lopside glanced over to Roro, slumped up against a watchful Daisy.

"She's still very weak," Lopside said. "Can't it wait?"

"We've already waited. We should ask her now."

Champion wasn't using any of her dominating postures or gestures. She didn't have to. She was right, and Lopside knew it.

"Ask me what?" Roro said. Grimacing, she raised herself on her elbows.

The dogs slunk over to her. They felt guilty for talking about her behind her back. But Lopside gave her a direct, challenging gaze.

"Ask me what?" she said again.

"We need to know why you left us," Lopside said. "Why you and the crew evacuated the *Laika*. Why you abandoned us."

Roro lay back down. She covered her eyes with her forearm, as if the minimal light from the overhead lamp was too bright.

"Of course you're wondering about that," Roro said. "Who could blame you for thinking you were left to die? Oh, my lovely dogs. Oh, you poor things."

She took a sip of water and closed her eyes a moment. Gathering her strength, or gathering her courage?

"We were in the arrival preparation stage for reaching HD 24040" she began. "The automatic systems brought us—by 'us,' I mean the human crew—out of hibernation. The *Laika* was exactly where she was supposed to be, right on the edge of the planetary system, and running perfectly. We had started to bring you dogs out of hibernation.

"And then . . ." She closed her eyes for so long Lopside thought she'd fallen asleep, but she opened them and continued. "I felt a great shudder and a whoosh of air. You know what that means. Something had breached the hull. A meteoroid. It became clear pretty quickly that the *Laika* was fatally damaged, and Commander Lin gave the order: Abandon ship."

Her voice shuddered, and Lopside almost called a stop to this. It wasn't just the telling of the story that was costing her, but the story itself. She took another sip of water and continued.

"I can't blame the commander. His job was to fulfill the mission and protect the crew. He knew better than anyone that the ship and the mission were lost, so he kept to his orders: Save the crew. We were all supposed to board the lifepod and try to limp the rest of the way to Stepping Stone."

"But without us," Champion said.

"You know coming out of hibernation takes hours," Roro said. "Do it too quickly, and the subject goes into shock and dies. And the hibernation beds are completely integrated into the ship systems. We couldn't take them with us. The commander felt he had to leave you behind. He didn't have much choice."

She closed her eyes again. When she opened them, Lopside saw a steely resolve.

"I disobeyed orders. Because . . . I just couldn't." Her

voice thickened, and her eyes glistened. "I couldn't leave you by yourselves. I had to try. Instead of boarding the lifepod, I grabbed a survival suit and a tank of emergency repair foam and headed for the airlock. As I exited the ship, I watched the lifepod accelerate away from the *Laika*."

"You stayed behind and sealed the breach," Lopside said. "I saw it the first time I went out in the Rover to fix the communications antenna."

Roro swallowed and wiped her eyes. "Yes."

"But why didn't you come back inside the ship?"

"Commander Lin sent out a grappling drone. It grabbed me and reeled me in. I begged him to leave me behind, to let me get back inside the *Laika*. I knew he wouldn't. But the thought of leaving you . . . of abandoning you . . ."

Her voice trailed off. Daisy gave Champion a hard look. "She's tired."

Champion returned Daisy's look with a soft one.

"Roro, what happened to the lifepod?"

Roro licked her cracked lips and swallowed some more water. "We lasted a couple of weeks. Made it as far as the asteroid field before one of the smaller asteroids hit us. The crew were sucked out into space. Engineer Lopez. Medical

Officer Ortega. Commander Lin. All of them." Her voice was barely a whisper now. "All but me. I was near the suit lockers, and I was the only one who managed to get my survival suit on before the lifepod broke up around me. I tried to reach the others, to help them into suits . . . but they scattered. Like confetti in the wind. They were gone."

"She has to rest," Daisy insisted. Lopside was ready to agree with her, but Roro waved a hand.

"No. This is my mission report, and you're my crew-mates. I'll finish telling you. I used every ounce of my suit's propellant to steer me to the asteroid where Lopside found me. Made contact with the surface and woke up at the bottom of the crater. My water and oxygen recycler worked, and I had my emergency beacon. But, honestly, I didn't have much hope. I thought it was just a matter of time until my battery gave out and I froze to death."

"You almost did," Champion said.

"Almost," she agreed. "But I held on to a tiny shred of hope. Just a morsel. I kept thinking, If there's a way the dogs can find me, they will. I guess hoping was the right strategy."

Champion came forward. She bent her face down and

gave Roro's hand a gentle lick. Bug did the same. And then Daisy, slopping her wet tongue over Roro's fingers.

"You didn't abandon us," Lopside said. "You didn't abandon us, and we didn't abandon you." He touched his nose to hers. "Dogs and people. Together."

TWENTY-FIVE

THEY LET RORO SLEEP THROUGH most of the next day. Daisy woke her up just often enough to make her nibble on an ERP and drink water and electrolytes. Meanwhile, Bug and Champion and Lopside went over their situation again. They were happy beyond barks that they'd gotten Roro back, but every other dilemma remained unchanged. They were still adrift with vanishing power and supplies, and they still had no way to make the distance to Stepping Stone within a dog or human lifespan.

"Are you sure you can't do anything with the singularity core I recovered from the lifepod?" Lopside asked again for the fifth time.

Bug yawned with irritation.

"It's worthless without the other half of the Tesseract motor: the anti-graviton generator. And for all we know, this core is just as unstable as the one that destroyed the *Laika*. We should probably jettison it out into space, just to be safe."

Daisy ambled over. "The dome's gravity generator is what keeps us from floating off the deck, right? So why can't we reverse it or whatever to make anti-gravitons and then hook up the singularity core to make a Tesseract motor and use the Tesseract motor to get us the rest of the way to Stepping Stone, and I know you're not supposed to use a Tesseract motor inside a planetary system because it's dangerous and everything could go bad and awful and wrong, but everything's already bad and awful and wrong and maybe it *won't* go bad and awful and wrong and that way we won't die in space and I'll get to run in the grass on the planet."

Lopside and the other dogs just stared at her. Their jaws hung open. They cocked their heads.

"Bug?" Champion said. "Is this even possible?"

"I . . . I . . . ," Bug said.

"It could work!" Roro came over on stiff legs. She was

still weak, but she wore a huge grin. "Daisy . . . you're a genius!"

"I know," Daisy said with a haughty sniff. "Nobody gets that about me. Anyway, I just came over to tell you all the eggs are hatching."

Lopside still hadn't closed his jaw or uncocked his head. "Are you sure, Daisy?"

"Well, I could be wrong. I mean, there's little cracks in them that weren't there before. And some of them have little holes. And I think I can see the tips of tiny little chicken beaks sticking out of the holes. But I'm not an expert."

Lopside dashed over to the blanket nest. Tiny beaks appeared through holes in some of the eggs. And among the remains of a shell, a wet pink-and-yellow blob struggled to move, peeping for its mother.

It was almost precisely four weeks since Lopside had taken the chicken eggs from the broken EggHab. Four weeks of disasters, of evacuations, of cracked domes and unstable singularities and extravehicular canine rescues. It seemed like so much longer.

Lopside lowered his nose, slowly, carefully. He gave the chick a sniff.

"Don't you worry, little chicken," he said. "This mission isn't over yet."

Bug and Lopside and Champion spent sleepless hours getting into the guts of the gravity generators. Roro worked furiously on her tablet, figuring out how to redirect the gravity emitters so they would push instead of pull.

Even more complicated was the task of hooking up the singularity core. But following Roro's instructions and working their paw pads raw, the dogs were finally able to tighten the last fastener and close the last hatch.

Along with directing them through the mechanical work, Roro also figured out the launch window. Stepping Stone was in constant motion around the star, so Roro had to calculate the right time to activate the cobbled-together Tesseract motor so the dome and the planet would meet up in space.

There was no sense of relief when Roro completed her calculations.

"I've figured out the launch window," she said. "We have ten minutes."

Bug's eyes bugged out. "But . . . we're not ready. We need to run more tests. What if I got something wrong?"

"Ten minutes isn't enough," agreed Champion. "When's the next launch window after that?"

Roro consulted her tablet and checked her watch. "One hundred and seventy-three years."

"Sorry, Bug," Champion said. "We don't have time for more tests. But we all have confidence in your work."

"I don't have confidence in my work," Bug barked back. "One press of the button could kill us. We could be blasted apart. We could implode. We could be crushed, or splatted into kibble and jam."

Daisy rolled around on the ground. "I don't want to be kibble and jam."

"I don't think we have much choice," Roro said. Her voice remained calm, but Lopside could hear how hard her heart was beating. "We fire the anti-gravitons now and risk death, or we never reach Stepping Stone."

"We don't know that," Bug said. "We might figure out how to get the thrusters back online. We might find a way to get more power from the batteries. There's still time."

Lopside felt for Bug. Bug didn't want to be responsible for killing his pack. Nobody did. Lopside could even smell Champion's hesitation. He was so happy not to be pack leader right now.

"Champion," he said, wanting to lift some of the weight off her shoulders. "Call for a vote."

"Do it fast," Roro said. "The clock's ticking."

Back in the old times, before the hull breach, before the crew abandoned the *Laika*, any human would be considered higher ranking than any dog. But Roro didn't presume she should make all the decisions. They were all part of the same pack, and Roro recognized that she wasn't pack leader.

Champion cleared her throat. She shook off nervous energy and then adopted her best Champion pose.

"All in favor of pushing the button—"

She didn't get all the words out before Lopside and Daisy raised their right paws. Champion raised her own paw.

"That's three out of the five of us," Roro said. "A majority. And I'm with you." She raised her right hand.

Bug growled. "We're probably going to die, but we might as well make it unanimous. Barkonauts, together." His paw went up.

At the control panel, Roro rolled up her sleeve, her finger hovering over the button that would either get them to Stepping Stone or kill them in a very unpleasant way.

"Wait," said Champion. "Lopside is the member of this

crew most responsible for reminding us that our job is to complete our mission. There were times I felt like quitting, but Lopside wouldn't let me, even when I was trapped under a hatch with a broken leg. I think he should have the honor of pushing the button."

Bug and Daisy wagged their tails in agreement.

Lopside didn't know what to say, but he managed to bark out, "Thanks."

Roro reached down and lifted him to the top of the control panel. She patted his back and scritched behind his ears, and Lopside lifted his fateful paw over the button.

"Together," he said, bringing his paw down.

EPILOGUE

LOPSIDE LAY IN THE SUN, warming his belly in the purple grass. A gentle breeze rustled long-stemmed flowers that didn't yet have a name. The air smelled of spicy tree bark and rich, fungal earth. It smelled damp and green and strange and wonderful.

A few yards off, chickens clucked and scratched in the dirt. And off on a hill not too far in the distance, calves and lambs and goat kids grazed with the flash of Bug's black-and-white-and-tan fur weaving among their legs. The occasional bleat or moo of complaint rang out when Bug took a nip at an ankle.

Bug was having the time of his life, but he was still

doing his job, and Lopside felt a bit guilty for lazing about. Besides, it was almost time for the pack to gather. He got up and stretched, put his nose to the ground, and sniffed for rats.

He had not yet found a rat, or anything like a rat, in the five years since the *Laika*'s dome had set down on the planet. But he hadn't given up. Stepping Stone was a big, rich, wild world. There had to be rats somewhere.

It had been a rough landing. A landing that cracked the dome glass and smashed the gravity generators. But, as Roro had said, any landing you can walk away from is a good landing.

They didn't need the gravity generators anyway. Stepping Stone had gravity of its own.

Lopside crossed the meadow to the shore of the fish pond. He called out to Champion, who was paddling across the water. Her smile of mad joy was infectious, and Lopside wagged his tail at her.

Most of the plants and bugs and hills and other land features on the planet didn't have names yet, but the pond did. It was the very first thing they named, and they called it Lake Laika. And on its shore was a high stack of stones:

a memorial to the *Laika*'s fallen crew. The stones were stained with pee, left by the pack as a sign of respect and remembrance.

"Is it time?" Champion barked.

"Just about."

Champion swam to shore and shook water off her coat, soaking Lopside in the process. Lopside tried to bite her tail in retaliation, but Champion was too fast for him. She barked a laugh and sprinted off toward the dome. Lopside followed, and Bug left the livestock behind to join them.

They smelled and heard Daisy before they saw her, a great galloping commotion sending up clouds of butterfly-like insects with silver wings the size of dinner plates. She ran for miles every day. She wasn't a puppy anymore, but no amount of exercise could ever curb her energy. She rolled in dirt the color of boysenberries until Roro came out of the dome.

The dogs swarmed her and demanded pets and scritches as if they hadn't seen her in forever. They greeted her the same way every time, even if the last time they'd seen her had been five minutes ago.

Roro was filthy, dirt smearing her knees and cheeks. She'd been in the dome, tending the season's crops. With the wild vegetables and grains she cultivated, and the fish that lived in Lake Laika, the pack was well fed.

Roro checked her watch and pointed to the sky. "Right on schedule," she said.

Lopside followed the direction of her finger and spotted what she was pointing at.

There was a light in the daytime sky, brighter than any star. It was getting brighter, and it was falling: the second mission to Stepping Stone.

Twenty human crew members. Two more cows, six more sheep, six more goats, twelve more chickens. And eight more dogs.

No rats, as far as Lopside knew, but he would never stop hoping.

ACKNOWLEDGMENTS

LIKE THE BARKONAUTS OF THE *Laika*, I depended on a whole pack of friends and colleagues to get this book all the way to its destination. Always first and foremost, thanks to my loving ground control, Lisa Will. In addition to constant support, Lisa provided her expertise as an astrophysicist to point out scientific errors and impossibilities in my story, and if any remain, they are entirely my fault.

Heartfelt thanks to my agent, Holly Root, who signed me as a client when I was a bit of a lost stray and who believed in my book, perhaps more than I did.

And my deepest respect and gratitude to my editor, Erica Sussman, who made this book so much better by asking the right questions and navigating me to the best answers; to Deanna Hoak, copy editor extraordinaire, for making me look good; Mark Frederickson for his cover and interior illustration that so well captures the essence of *dog*; Aurora Parlagreco for her beautiful book design; and Oliver Burston for the fantastic logo design. And to all the editorial, production, sales, marketing, publicity, and administrative crew at HarperCollins, thank you for everything you did to get this book into shape and launch it on its voyage.

Members of my own personal pack read the manuscript in early form, gave me encouragement and advice and cheered me on. To Tobias Buckell, Rae Carson, Deb Coates, C.C Finlay, Alan Gratz, Karen Meisner, Sandra McDonald, Sarah Prineas, thank you all. And a special thanks to Jenn Reese for naming my crew the Barkonauts.

Finally, to the pooches everywhere, without whom humans would be a very different and poorer species: You're all good dogs.

Love dogs?
You may also like...